CAMUS CALLING

Jessie MacQuarrie

Jessie MacQuarrie

ISBN: 978-1-909424-68-5

For Garry, my rock, who makes everything possible.

FINDING CAMUS

THOSE WHO ARE aware of the history of Scotland will be familiar with the sad, dark days of the highland clearances. The west coast, and in particular the Western Isles, saw many hardy folk forced away across rough seas either to the mainland or perhaps even further afield to Canada and Nova Scotia. It is easy to picture those grey days with eyes wet with a mixture of sea spray and tears, yet today is a complete contrast.

In recent times there has been a marked increase in tourism in Britain. In particular a number of television programmes have focused on areas of Scotland which offer scenery and wildlife not seen by most sitting in front of their plasma screens. The effect has been noticeable. More and more visitors are coming. Britons themselves, fed up with the hustles of airport travel and unpredictable exchange rates, are looking to areas of Britain which offer beauty, peace, tranquillity and above all else a complete absence of heavy traffic, noisy crowded bars, sun beds adorned with German towels and empty McDonald's boxes!

Reg and Phyllis are approaching their sixth season as wardens of the Camus site. It is late March. The site is due to open on 1st April and much needs to be done. The air is cold and crisp but the sky is clear and blue. The sound of oyster catchers fills the air and busy pairs can be seen foraging in the kelp lined up along the shore. Looking across the sound, the now empty islands rise from the sea awaiting the return of seabirds to their nests with their newly acquired catch of the day. A familiar dishevelled looking heron is poised motionless for his next catch. It is hard to resist the temptation to linger and watch but Reg has a long schedule of tasks which now needs to be set in motion in preparation for the start of the new season.

Reg is now 67. He was born in Portsmouth and started as a young boy in the dockyard working on many naval ships and submarines. At the age of 21 he applied to the army and progressed to become a Warrant Officer, a position he held for 30 years. To adequately describe Reg it is without doubt best to refer to the army's own definition:

> *'An officer appointed by warrant by the Secretary of the Army, based upon a sound level of technical and tactical competence. The Warrant Officer is the highly specialized expert and trainer, who, by gaining progressive levels of expertise and leadership, operates, maintains, administers, and manages the Army's equipment, support activities, or technical systems for an entire career'.*
> *(Para 1-5, Army Regulation 611-112)*

Reg and Phyllis share a passion for caravans and their 25 years of caravanning holidays so it seemed only natural that, upon retirement, they considered applying to become wardens of a caravan site. It seemed that early 60s was too soon for full retirement and the chance to combine their passion for caravanning with an opportunity to supplement their retirement fund was worth pursuing. Their first application was for a site in the West Country. Phyliss was quite taken by this location as the climate would be likely to be kind to her other passion for flowers and hanging baskets. Unfortunately the warden positions were keenly sought after and they were not successful either for the West Country site or the next four positions for which they applied. Reg's background surely made him an ideal candidate. As a Warrant Officer he had demonstrated good, organisational skills for example he had once trained, advised and led a whole platoon of soldiers across Rannoch Moor in the depth of winter. He had used his technical skills to build temporary accommodation, erect fences and fix numerous broken army vehicles. Surely there was no task involved in running and maintaining a caravan site that was beyond him.

When Phyllis once again scoured the magazines for any new opportunities, she came across the position advertised for wardens for the Camus site. She called Reg in from the garden and made a nice cup of tea.

" I've found another site" she said with excitement.

Reg pulled out his well used map book from its allotted space on the book shelf and proceeded to pinpoint exactly where Kilchoan was. It was on the western coast of Scotland on the mainland between Oban and Mallaig.

"It's well off the beaten track" he revealed. "I'll search on the internet once I've had my tea."

He soon discovered that the weather on the west coast was not known for its kindness. On average there are 193 days of rain, that's more than half a year. Being on the coast, the winds coming in from the Atlantic can be fierce and the temperature is significantly cooler than can be found in the West Country. They sat and discussed whether they should apply. They both agreed that whilst it might not be the most idyllic location, they should apply anyway and wait and see what happened. Possibly other applicants were similarly deterred as several weeks later a letter came asking them to complete a formal application form. Given that, the form ran to several pages Reg naturally took charge.

"I'll fill in most of the form dear. There's only three questions which would be best left to you." Reg assumed his usual role but after nearly 40 years of marriage Phyllis simply let him take control.

Besides the usual questions relating to names, address, dates of birth etc there were specific questions relating to caravan experience, towing skills, building, plumbing and drainage and experience relating to grounds maintenance. Reg had various certificates earned throughout his career, for example first aid, safety at work and storage of firearms but most of them dated back at least 15 years so he fully expected that the modern demands of Health and Safety would require him to undergo further training. Phyliss answered her three questions which asked for her views on the importance of presentation around the reception area, her experience of ordering stock for the site shop and her computer skills relating to the booking system. Fortunately she had previously been a secretary to a company director and had continued her use of the internet on into retirement. She completed her allocated questions with ease.

They sent off their application the day after it arrived and sat back to await a response. Two weeks later a letter came through the post asking them to attend an interview at the 'Touring Haven Holiday' head offices. What should they wear? Would it be best to go dressed informally, demonstrating their ability to get stuck in? Reg had a smart pair of blue overalls which were well suited to taking on any task. Alternatively he could go in his smart trousers with his blazer adorned with his military ribbons. Perhaps that would impress.

The day of the interview came and Reg had decided that formal was best so they dressed in their best and headed for the office. Phyliss was nervous and, as she always tended to talk incessantly, Reg had decided that he should take control and that she should only answer questions directed specifically at her.

"Oh I've got butterflies in my stomach. I feel like I did when I sat my exams" she told Reg, who was, as always, irritatingly calm and collected.

To their surprise they were led into separate rooms and interviewed by different members of staff. Phyliss soon struck up a friendly rapport with the lady interviewing her and they exchanged experiences of caravan holidays past. Reg seemed to take a lot longer as he had a wealth of experience which he was determined to reveal. He was able to give many examples of technical achievements, organisational and, in particular, people skills. The fact that Reg was in the room for almost an hour gave Phyllis plenty of time to find out more about the role of warden and she was brimming with enthusiasm when they both emerged.

Whatever they said must have impressed. A week later they received the response they had hoped for: the position was theirs.

It was now November and they were due to start by 1st March in the following year. The site had a specific pitch for the wardens' own caravan. When the site was open they would be expected to stay there but what to do in the closed season was now to be considered.

They considered whether to sell their immaculate bungalow in Worcestershire after all it would be empty from March to November. Who would tend to their much loved garden and what would be the cost of keeping it empty? Somehow it felt a bit premature to put it on the market. After all what if they didn't like their new lives as wardens? They quickly decided to keep it for the time being and look again at the end of their first season.

Phyllis spent a considerable time on the phone telling friends all about their new venture. She had surely told them all the same details several times over! Reg simply retreated to his shed taking the necessary time for essential planning!

There was still a lot of organising to do between now and March. First there was Christmas to prepare for, presents to buy, friends and family to see and bid farewell to but most important and most pressing was to organise a visit to the site and get a feel for what awaited them. It was already into November so they quickly decided to drive there and spend a couple of days in a B&B to get a feel for the place.

It was to be a long drive of about 470 miles so they prepared their sandwiches and a flask and set out early in order to arrive in daylight. Reg made sure that he had a clipboard, pen and paper, torch and camera to hand so that he could make a full record of his inspection and obtain all the information needed to make preparations. He had previously fully prepared himself with the AA route planner's map and directions. They were both really excited as they started out on this new venture.

The route took them north just past Glencoe to a small ferry. From then on it was west towards the coast. The road through Glencoe was awesome. The towering mountains on either side looked somewhat frightening.

"Although it's beautiful there's something quite eerie about this place" said Phyllis "This is the place of the famous massacre isn't it?".

"Yes indeed" replied Reg.

In reality he was concentrating on the steep twisting road. They were currently in their car with nothing behind and yet the terrain required considerable concentration. They were already imagining towing their caravan in a few months' time. It was already 3.30pm and the light had almost disappeared. They had not taken into account how quickly the darkness falls this far north. There was still a fair way to go and they became increasingly worried that it could be hard to find their way.

Once across the ferry they were into even remoter country. It was certainly peaceful and beautiful. Fortunately the sky was clear and the full moon was shedding some light as if to show the way. The road seemed to twist and turn endlessly and added to their tiredness. The hassle of the earlier part of the journey seemed long ago. Other cars were now few and far between but so too were any welcoming lights of homes, shops or garages indicating that not many others had also ventured this far. Eventually the road narrowed to a single track with an occasional twinkle of light between the branches of the trees.

Reg put on the courtesy light so that Phyliss could read the local directions provided by Meg the owner of the B&B in which they had planned to stay. The directions were good and they finally arrived at the converted steading aptly named Taigh Meg.

"Failte" she announced as she opened the door "so good to see you both. Come in you've had a long journey"

Phyllis hadn't caught her first word spoken in a soft but welcoming tone and assumed that it was a local dialect. Meg made them a lovely fresh pot of tea and sat them by the wood burner before showing them their room. They had not considered what they might eat that evening assuming that there would be a restaurant or pub close by but Meg knew better and had already prepared a big pot of stovies for their arrival. They accepted her offer graciously, not having a clue what 'stovies' might be. Meg soon explained that stovies was a traditional hearty Scots meal made from potatoes, onions and left over meat served as a stew. It certainly smelt good after that long journey and as they all sat round the table the conversation soon flowed.

Reg and Phyliss were anxious to ask Meg all about the area and whether she knew anything about the caravan site. Meg had lived there for over 50 years and was therefore an endless source of information. As a girl she had grown up in the village across the hills. Her husband, now sadly departed, had worked on the Ferry which ran from the pier before he died two years ago. Her children had grown up and moved away to Glasgow in search of work and city life. Meg was therefore on her own so had started to offer B&B. She did of course enjoy the company and was so pleased to find out that Phyliss loved to chat.

"Och I suppose that the site was opened about eight years ago" Meg revealed. "I met each of the previous wardens but they always seemed busy and were only at Camus from March to October. Several only stayed the one season. I didn't really feel that I got to know them. They always seemed pleased to return home." Meg sounded quite disappointed. Would Reg and Phyllis be any different? "Perhaps the weather had put them off after all last year was a particularly disappointing summer".

Reg asked her about the name of the site 'Camus' and what it meant.

"Camus is Gaelic for bay" she said " the curved coastline has harboured many a fishing boat over the years offering, along with the offshore islands added protection from the fierce waters blown across the Atlantic."

"So where will our visitors find local places to eat and drink?" asked Reg.

Meg smiled and proudly gave them details of the Ferry Boathouse where her husband used to work and the tea room at Ardnamurchan Point lighthouse. Of course there was 'The Dobhran' an inn in the village 10 miles away which is the Gaelic word for otter. They served home cooked food in the evenings but she hadn't been there for a long time so couldn't be sure if it had changed hands. She extolled the virtues of the Ferry Boathouse which specialised in seafood caught, landed and prepared by Joyce, the ferryman's wife. Joyce was her closest friend and had been so good to her since her husband had died. What Joyce couldn't do with a freshly caught crab! Mind you the Boathouse only served food during the ferry operating times, which varied according to the season.

Reg was anxious to know where the nearest shops were. He was conscious that they hadn't passed any on his route from the ferry to the B&B. Meg told them that the nearest supermarket was back on the mainland but the local village store had a good stock of essential supplies and that was only 20 minutes from the Camus site. Meg always referred to the other side of the ferry they had crossed as 'the mainland'. Although her village was still connected by road it was a journey of over 40 miles and all the local people considered that they were effectively an island.

Reg was tired after such a long drive. "If you don't mind ladies I think that I'll take myself to bed. We've lots to do tomorrow" he said, politely excusing himself.

He was already harbouring anxious thoughts about the caravan site and whether people would want to come this far. He was concerned about the absence of shops and added one more task to his list before retiring to bed. He would need to ensure that he had a good shop on site and would need to stock it with essential supplies. He may even have to build a shop if there wasn't already one there.

Phyliss stayed up talking to Meg for another hour. Their conversation moved from details of their children to their bungalow in Worcester and whether they should sell it. Meg had various stories about guests who had already stayed at her B&B and how many visitors she was expecting this year. She was very independent and resourceful, an essential quality for a highland widow but she gratefully accepted Phyliss's kind offer for Reg to lend a hand as they would only be a few miles down the road.

WHAT WAS IN STORE?

THE NEXT MORNING Meg had made them a fine breakfast of porridge followed by poached eggs from her own hens. Reg and Phyllis had an itinerary for the day so Reg was keen to get going. Meg had made arrangements for a meal that evening which they were once again glad to accept. She had also made them a flask of home made soup and some freshly baked bread to see them through the day. Phyllis was impressed with her offer of freshly baked bread it was apparent to her that these highland folk were well used to self sufficiency. Perhaps she would need to extend her skills beyond hanging baskets!

The caravan site was a further three miles down the single-track road which soon hugged the shoreline. They couldn't see much as there was mist across the sea, just a few boats looking deserted and listing up onto the shore. Just before they reached the site, there was a quaint humped-back bridge which crossed the burn running out to sea. They did not foresee the dramas that this picturesque scene would reveal in the season to come.

Reg had put on his blue boiler suit with not only his trusty thermal underwear underneath but also several layers of jumpers and jackets over the top. Of course he had brought his visi-jacket with him just in case!

They arrived at the rusty old gates and Reg took the set of keys from the glove box. He had been given a full set by the 'Touring Haven Holiday' offices and had brought with him some adhesive strip in order to clearly make up labels to indicate what each key was for. He tried several before successfully turning the key in the padlock and ceremoniously pulled back the gates. Phyllis was keen to get out and explore but the wind was biting so she hastily grabbed a second jacket, some gloves and her bobble hat before venturing out.

Apart from the sound of seagulls and oyster catchers ringing out from the shore there was otherwise silence - no traffic noise, no people. It was only 10.30 in the morning and they both hoped that the mist would clear later on so that they could get a better feel for the site and surroundings. For now they would have to concentrate on the site itself.

Reg studied his list which he had prepared at home. His first task was to check the number and state of the pitches. They had stayed on many caravan sites over the last 25 years. Of course, when they started out caravan sites were often farmers' fields but now the discerning caravanner expected more. Nowadays many pitches were clear to see and a lot were hard-standing. So they started their walkabout, with Reg and his clipboard to the ready.

The pitches were not clearly marked at all but the positioning of the electric hook-up points was a clue. Reg quickly decided that the best way to start was to draw up a sketch of the site and therefore passed the clipboard to Phyllis to hold whilst he measured by counting his own extended paces as he marched around the site. Phyllis followed behind passing the sketch to Reg so that he could add the exact distances between each noted point. There were several features which were obvious. There was a reception, a toilet/shower block, two large sheds, a slipway to the shore and even a boathouse. All of these buildings were worthy of thorough examination as detailed further down Reg's list. Phyllis was excited and kept pointing things out to Reg but he soon became irritated.

"Do be quiet Phyllis" he said "You're putting me off my counting!"

Collecting the measurements for his sketch took a good half hour but at least they could now take note of the pitches and their location. None of the pitches were the up-to-date hard-standing with manicured gravel. They were all on a mixture of grass interspersed with rocks and stones. From the electric hook-up points, Reg made out that there was capacity for 26 caravans, assuming of course that they all worked. He had not planned to check each hook-up until they were due to return in March. Of these pitches, Reg noted that half would have a clear sea view except that today, there was still no such view, as the mist had still not cleared and it was already midday.

The next task was to explore the various buildings and see what they had inherited from the previous wardens.

Firstly the reception. Reg juggled with the set of keys he had. Phyllis could see that it was at least built of brick and looked fairly solid although the window frames had not weathered very well. It looked a reasonable size but was so drab that it certainly cried out to be festooned in her best hanging baskets. Reg tried a couple of keys and once inside he was keen to make up the required label. The reception had a spacious counter with shelves underneath and at the far end was ample space which they thought could be used for information leaflets, postcards etc. At the back were a toilet and sink and a useful store cupboard. Reg made full use of his note book and pulled out his retractable tape measure to record the exact details. He tried the light switch but there was either no power or the bulb had blown. He was cross that he hadn't bought a spare bulb with him. How could he have not put one in the car! Luckily he had brought his torch!

They decided to take a short break for lunch. Phyllis was particularly looking forward to the home-made bread and soup that Meg had kindly packed for them. The soup had lost that piping hot temperature in spite of being in a thermos but it was at least still warm and the bread was delicious.

"It was really kind of Meg to prepare this lunch for us. It's all home-made you know" Phyllis said with real appreciation and a hint of admiration.

"She's a fair cook" replied Reg "Just as well as I haven't seen much sign of anywhere else where we might have bought something."

After only a short break of fifteen minutes, which Reg had pre-allocated in his schedule for the day, it was time to continue their inspection.

They had wondered what they would find in the way of a toilet block and had conjured up images of their earlier caravanning experiences. Phyllis had memories of draughty, trickling, cold showers full of spiders and toilets which invariably refused to flush. Reg on the other hand was used to army life, even digging his own toilet if necessary. These days though people expect higher standards so they both approached nervously, knowing that times had moved on since those old days. Once again the building was made of brick and looked relatively recent. 'Adequate' was the best initial description. The ladies had three WCs, two showers and three sinks. The men's was similarly equipped. It looked a little dirty but had obviously been shut up for many months now so that wasn't surprising.

They moved on to the two sheds, wondering what they would find inside. Reg was particularly excited at the thoughts of tools and machinery that might prove useful in days to come. The first shed was painted green and constructed of corrugated metal, the other must have been an old steading or barn and was very old indeed. The base was built from rocks covered with years of moss. Reg was sure that the stones had been laid by hand many generations ago. How hard these old crofters must have worked to construct this. They would not have had the tools and heavy lifting equipment in use today. He was mindful to ask Meg later if she knew anything of the history of this site.

Reg was lured first to the old steading. He was as much intrigued about the structure as he was with what it might reveal inside. There was no need for him to fumble with the assortment of keys as it was merely sealed by an old wooden door which required a good nudge to free it from the rotting frame. It must have swelled from its attempt to keep out the driving rain. The steading was dark inside as it only had two small windows to let in any light indeed one of them was broken. In the darkness Reg used his torch and could make out an old tractor which looked like it had not been used for a long time, two petrol driven mowers and numerous farming/gardening tools such as spades, brushes, rakes etc. Phyllis poked her head inside but was reluctant to venture further due to her fear of spiders and any other crawly creatures. A strange noise came from the roof but it was too dark to see what it was. Phyllis went back outside - she would leave the rest to Reg. He would have gladly stayed in the steading for hours but he was conscious that there were more items on his list which all needed to be ticked before the light was lost.

And so to the last shed. Inside revealed a useful workshop with a long wooden bench complete with a vice, saws, screwdrivers, chisels and boxes of nails and screws. The workshop suggested that there was both power and light and Reg used his torch to investigate the electrical box above the bench. He found the switch and flicked it on. To his delight the power was on and, at last, he was able to get a better look around. At the back of the shed were various containers, all labelled. Reg quickly assessed that these related to cleaning and chemical waste. This would be a useful start when they took over in March. There was also a whole collection of dustbins which had been collected from around the site and safely stored to prevent them from blowing around and probably ending up out to sea. In one dustbin was a large amount of pellets but no clear marking. Reg could smell that they were some sort of animal feed but couldn't imagine what they were doing in a campsite shed - after all there were no animals on the site inventory.

It was now nearly 3 o'clock and the light was beginning to fade so they made their way to the slipway and the boathouse. The slipway might offer guests the chance to venture out in a dinghy or even a canoe. Reg was already considering investing in some appropriate equipment. As they came close, something ran across the slipway and disappeared in to the water. They couldn't see what it was but stood for a while to see if it reappeared. It didn't. The boathouse had seen better days and if it was to be used would need some sturdy repairs which Reg was confident he could do. Just up on the beach were a few old nets and lobster pots but they looked like they had not caught anything for years. After finding the old tractor Reg was hoping that it might be complemented by an old boat maybe a rowing boat or a small sailing boat. No such luck. From peering through the numerous cracks in the broken, wooden structure he could see that it was disappointingly empty. The sound of lapping water echoed inside but nevertheless the boathouse's addition to the site was a real bonus.

Reg was keen to at least take a quick tour around the immediate area. It was so dark the previous evening and they were due to leave and go back home first thing the following morning. The light was not going to hold out much longer but at least, if they were quick, they could make the best use of the remaining light. They made sure that everything was securely locked, being so used to life further south, and then returned to their car and headed off away from the B&B to see what lay further along the coast.

A few highland cattle were grazing just by the roadside. Phyllis thought that these iconic beasts were wonderful and would be loved by any visitors to the site. It was still difficult to see much offshore which was a real shame as they had hoped to enjoy the fine views which the caravan holiday staff had told them about. Perhaps Meg might have some photos to show them. They passed only a few small, isolated houses before they decided to return to the B&B. What a fruitful day they had had. Phyllis talked non-stop on the short journey back about her thoughts and plans and in particular her intentions for the reception and the hanging baskets.

It was only 4.30pm when they got back to Meg's. She made them a nice pot of tea and sat down to hear all about their findings.

"The reception will look so much more welcoming when I hang my baskets. I have lots of begonia tubers in the greenhouse at home which I will bring on in the spring. I've got Babylon, Pastel Cascade, Orange, White and my favourite, Picotee Ruffled Lace. Do you do your own baskets?" she asked Meg hoping that she might share her enthusiasm.

"Yes I do a few baskets to welcome my B&B guests but, up here, they're not usually ready until early June" replied Meg.

Reg didn't really listen to their conversation. His own head was awash with his findings. Had he remembered everything on his list? Had he got enough information written down to allow for the next stage of his preparations?

They told Meg everything they had discovered but the mist had prevented them from seeing the views. Meg assured them that, on a clear day, you could see across the bay to the distant islands and told them that from June to the end of September you could catch the Ferry to the Isle of Mull which was truly beautiful. In addition to the Ferry a few independent locals were happy to take people on boat trips around the local coast. Her husband had worked on the Ferry since he was a young boy and had helped out on the smaller boats as well. She had gone with him several times and had never tired of the sea trips.

"There's always something quite magical and serene about the sea" she added. "I've seen dolphins, minke whales, seals, puffins and schools of fish."

She didn't have many recent photos but she went upstairs to find her treasured box. In it were photos of her husband aboard the ferry and her children when they were quite young, playing down by the shore. Reg asked her about the caravan site and was eager to find out its history. Meg said that over 20 years ago the site was part of an old croft belonging to Hamish who lived along the coast. He used to keep sheep and cattle there as it was not suitable for arable crops. About 10 years ago he had de-crofted and leased the land to the caravan company in order to provide a regular income for his old age. She wasn't sure how old the steading was. As far as she knew it had always been there. Hamish used to leave it open as a shelter for the animals but she thought that it had been there a lot longer and that it was thought to be a crofter's home before the Clearances. Phyllis was curious. She knew nothing about the 'Clearances'. Meg needed to put the vegetables on for dinner but agreed to return to the subject after their meal. It was a venison casserole that Meg had prepared and the whole cottage was filled with an inviting aroma. They made their way to their room to freshen up and prepare for their early departure in the morning. Reg wanted to be away by 7.30am if that was ok with Meg.

After dinner they continued to chat about their plans. They were due to return on 1st March with their caravan in which they would live throughout the season. Meg wondered how they would manage for such a long time in such a small space but Reg and Phyllis were experienced caravanners and were in fact looking forward to it. Their caravan was warm and comfortable with a TV and DVD player, a fridge and microwave, toilet, shower and even a fixed bed. Meg was surprised to hear how caravans had changed from her old perceptions.

A little later she returned to the earlier subject of the Clearances and it soon became obvious that she was quite passionate about it. The Clearances referred to the enforced move of people from the highlands and islands in the 1800s. These people had led a hard life in poor conditions and yet they were happy until the landowners wanted to replace them with sheep. Many families were forced to leave their homes and either accept a small plot on the mainland or even further afield across the Atlantic. Meg's own grandmother had been cleared from Eigg and she had many stories to recount. Phyllis was touched and absorbed by Meg's stories but once again Reg retired first as he faced a long drive home the following day.

ASSUME POSITION

THE 1ST MARCH came round really quickly. Once again Reg and Phyllis made the long journey north. With their caravan in tow they spread the journey over two days, stopping overnight just south of Carlisle. Once across the ferry the last leg of the journey was particularly an experience and it certainly called upon all the years of Reg's previous towing experience. However, at least this time, they knew where they were heading.

Just before the Camus site they had to negotiate the humped-back bridge. It was narrow and presented a real risk of grounding. Reg made sure that he approached at the right angle and took it very slowly. He would certainly make sure that all visitors were forewarned.

They arrived at the site just before 2pm and planned to set about preparing their own dedicated wardens' pitch. Unlike their visit in November, they had arrived on a beautiful crisp spring morning. As soon as Phyllis stepped out of the car the breathtaking views were apparent. For once she was completely speechless. The sky was clear and blue and looking out across the sea it would be easy to believe that they were in a Mediterranean country. The sea was calm with only the slightest ripples breaking on the shore. They could see across to the numerous islands all clearly within view. They knew that they had a considerable task ahead to prepare for their first season but already they were inspired by the beauty that lay before them.

Reg took great care in positioning and levelling his caravan. After all it was to be their home for the next eight months. It made sense to retain the wardens' pitch next to the reception enabling their guests to contact them when needed. The temptation to choose a new pitch close to the shore seemed unnecessary as they were now able to delight in the views every day as they went about their tasks.

Reg had already prepared a work schedule and Phyllis was looking forward to having responsibility for the reception. She had been very busy since Christmas, contacting the tourist office to request copies of all of the leaflets relating to local attractions. They had already sent her some maps and posters to display in her reception and she had been given the required stationery by the staff at 'Touring Haven Holidays'. They had given them an information pack specifically for wardens giving the necessary contact numbers if they had questions and also the procedures that they must follow in keeping with the standards required. Her over-wintered begonia tubas were already neatly stacked in trays which had been transported in the caravan. The bedding plants would be bought locally in time for the arrival of their first caravan. She had prepared a suggested list of items which would be stocked in the site shop including eggs, milk, bread, soups and sauces, sweets and crisps and of course the non-food items including shampoo, shower gel, paracetamol, stamps, postcards and batteries. This would all need to be sourced locally and Phyllis was looking forward to a return visit to Meg for suggestions.

Reg's schedule started with checking the site power supply followed by the outside stores. It was imperative to render these in order before ordering more supplies. The power supply to each of the buildings was working and fortunately the hook-up for the warden's pitch was fine too. It took him several days but he soon made sure that the green corrugated shed was in immaculate order. Any old unusable items were cleared away and the workbench was re-sanded and cleared for proper use. He applied a fresh coat of exterior paint and the dustbins were cleaned and prepared for strategic positioning around the site, all apart from the one containing the animal pellets which Reg was tempted to throw away but had decided to keep and give to a local farmer when he got the chance to meet him. So for now the pellets were transferred to the steading. Reg was itching to start organising the steading but had realised that the larger shed was best to tackle first. The individual electric hook-ups to each pitch needed attention but there was plenty of time to get them all ready for 1st April.

Phyllis and Reg soon became regular visitors to Meg's. Using Meg's local knowledge they had made plans with the local baker to deliver freshly baked bread every day. They would have to place the orders every week according to their expected visitor numbers but the baker was more than happy to add them to his customer round. These days it is difficult to order truly local milk. The industry is highly regulated but they had agreed to fetch it from the local village store. It is important in these rural communities to support other local traders. The round trip to the nearest supermarket was over 100 miles and was therefore not a convenient option other than perhaps monthly visits for non perishable items. It was also apparent that they themselves would need a large freezer for their own use. Perhaps a second freezer for their guests' needs was also a worthwhile investment.

Reg had planned to spend several days investigating the repairs required to the steading. Inside was not only the inviting tractor but also a ride-on mower, old fence posts and agricultural implements which he had only previously seen in museums. He waited for the dry days to get everything out. The weather was changeable. The morning might start overcast but the sun soon appeared. The rain was heavy but it could come and go in a flash. It was difficult for Reg to reliably plan his tasks for each day until he awoke each morning.

The tractor was an old Fordson, fairly rusty and with some bits missing but fortunately not beyond repair. This was excellent news because it was still possible to source replacement parts and buy various implements to attach. Reg gave Phyllis the job of seeking out likely suppliers on the internet. To start with Reg needed to push it out of the steading. As he was contemplating the best approach, he heard a warm greeting coming from the gate. It was the farmer from just along the coast who was passing and had therefore stopped to introduce himself.

"Hello there. You must be Reg. Meg told me all about you. I'm your neighbour Angus from just along the road."

He was a tall, strong looking man with a truly weather beaten face but a welcoming smile. He had a strong Scot's accent which meant that Reg had to concentrate hard to give the correct response.

"Pleased to meet you." Replied Reg shaking him by the hand. "Come to the van and meet Phyllis. You must stay for a cup of tea"

Reg showed him to the caravan which seemed even smaller when Angus sat down inside. Angus looked to be around 45 but it was hard to tell as his features were those of a man who worked outside in all weathers and might well be either older or considerably younger. Although it was more usually Phyllis who could talk for hours, Reg found himself particularly at ease with Angus and soon had given him a potted history of his earlier career and his build up to becoming the warden of the Camus site. Angus in turn explained that he was the son of Hamish who owned the croft along the coast. Hamish had retired and was now 82. He was still well but not as mobile as he might like therefore leaving Angus to tend to the sheep and cattle. To supplement the meagre returns from the croft Angus tended to his lobster pots every day unless the forecast was for winds above force six. His wife Elaine worked at home in the marketing industry. He and his family of three children live in a newly built house just along the coast. Angus had done most of the building work himself from digging the foundations to tiling the roof and only engaged help from a local electrician and plumber to check that the building met all the required standards for the purpose of signing off.

It was clear to Reg that Angus was a good all rounder and might prove a useful additional pair of hands if needed.

"You can always call on me if you need a hand" said Angus.

Reg sensed that the offer was genuine and quickly accepted assuring him that he would be able to pay him from the small budget he had been given to run the site. He also learned from Angus that his father still owned the land having leased it to Touring Haven holidays.

After their tea they both returned outside to get the old Fordson out of the steading. As they approached, Angus was proud to announce that it was his old and trusted friend which had served the croft well throughout his childhood. He knew it intimately and had fixed it many times before he acquired a more modern compact tractor to help with the site work when building his house. It had stopped working even before his father sold the land to the holiday company. Angus was delighted that Reg was intending to restore it and offered immediately to lend a hand. Angus's arrival proved particularly timely as Reg would have not been able to move it on his own. The tyres were flat and many parts had seized but Angus was big and strong and together they eventually managed to prise it from its temporary resting place and for the first time in many years it basked in the spring sunshine. He needed to get it out so that he could organise the steading and repair the broken window and roof trusses but Reg was also conscious that it would not fair well outside and un-protected so he used a tarpaulin to carefully preserve it from any further damage inflicted by the elements.

Angus had to get on and collect his lobster creels to see what he had caught but Reg had already struck up a good rapport with the man who would soon become a very close and trusted friend. On bidding Reg and Phyllis farewell he promised to check up on them any time he was passing and agreed to invite them to his home before the month was out.

It was noticeable that the days were much longer now and Reg was able to work into the early evening. He continued with the task at hand to clear a space in the old steading so that he could repair both the wooden door and the broken window. His intention was to run an armoured cable from the supply located in the other shed and calculated that he would need at least 100 metres. He therefore added this to his list but for now there was enough light for him to look up at the roof trusses with the additional help from his rechargeable torch. There were obvious signs of bird nesting material, straw and twigs hung from cobwebs in abundance. At the top of the roof was a particularly large nest but Reg couldn't make out whether it was still in use or a remnant from previous years. He made use of the remaining light organising the contents into obvious piles for further inspection the next day.

That night Reg went to bed with a warm feeling. He was already beginning to feel that life here would be everything he had imagined it to be. The time spent already with both Meg and Angus had made them feel that they were already making friends and being treated as part of a very close community and so far they had only been at Camus for one week. Reg hoped that this feeling would grow stronger as the passing weeks unfurled.

With only three weeks left until the site opened there still seemed to be so much to do. The pitches needed to be clearly marked out and rogue patches of growth needed to be cleared. Loose rocks and stones were set aside and each hook-up was tested and noted on Reg's schedule. Several required attention to the MCB trips.

Phyllis had already received bookings for the first three caravans arriving at the start of April. They worked hard through the rest of March with Reg using the old fence posts to contain the waste disposal areas and both of them spending hours sprucing up the toilet block. Phyllis chose new shower curtains and blinds and made the block feel warm and inviting. Reg made sure that the heating and hot water were in perfect order and when they were finished they felt quite proud of their achievement.

They had made several trips back to the mainland to fetch all the cleaning products, toilet rolls, soap etc and Reg had found a supplier for all his hardware, electrical and plumbing supplies. Their Ford Mondeo however was a bit of a squeeze when it came to picking up the larger supplies so they decided to invest some of their savings in an old jeep which could cope better especially when some of the roads were partially flooded. Reg was happy to have found a jeep in the traditional army green. It was over 10 years old but he was happy to fix any parts which needed replacing and what's more they had bought it for a fair price. It wasn't as comfortable as their ford saloon and it accentuated every pothole in the road but it was easy to load it up with all that they needed. Reg had chosen a jeep with a canvas back which could prove useful for transporting any large items with the canvas removed and yet has a cover of sorts which would protect their supplies from the frequent bursts of rain they would learn to expect.

Phyllis's was busy preparing her hanging baskets. The begonia tubas were now in pots in the reception. It would be a while until they popped up their heads and it was too early to expose them to the outside elements. The bedding plants which she had bought from the nursery just back over the ferry were much more expensive than those she was previously used to nurturing herself. She usually started all her plants from seed bringing them on in her greenhouse back in Worcester but this year it had not been possible apart from the begonias and she therefore consoled herself by giving her support the local businesses. She chose mature plants in a variety of colours ensuring that they would be a grand display to welcome their first visitors. She asked Reg to put up brackets on both sides of the reception door and also to make several long troughs that could be screwed to the boundary fence so as to create a colourful and welcoming feeling.

They set aside one day in each of the next three weeks to lay down their tools and explore the local area. It would obviously be important for them to be able to advise their guests of the best scenic tours, the best beaches and places to eat and drink. Their first trip was to fully explore the coastline. For the most part the single track road hugged the shore with several points which rose high up on cliffs giving far reaching views out to the small isles. They took endless photos which Phyllis intended to display in the reception as suggested places for guests to visit, picnic, walk and look out for wildlife. Angus had kindly also offered to take them out on his fishing boat to find the hidden coves not apparent to those travelling by car. Fortunately it was a calm clear day which pleased Phyllis who was afraid that she might suffer from sea sickness had the water been choppy. They had no idea how much wildlife was all around them. They had noticed the numerous sea birds but Angus could name each different species from oyster catchers to razor bills, cormorants, gannets and shanks. From his boat they could see seals popping their heads from the water.

"By the end of May we may well see dolphins. From June onwards, if you're lucky you could see minke whales and even the tell tale dorsal fin of a basking shark feeding just off the shore" Angus told them.

Phyllis returned to the site and immediately searched the internet to find posters and information about these creatures which she could display in the reception.

Another trip included a visit to the small ferry which Meg's late husband had crewed for many years. They had telephoned in advance and were once again made welcome by Joyce, the ferry man's wife, famous for her crab dishes according to Meg. Joyce's husband was Jimmy and he took Reg down to see the ferry which was his pride and joy.

"Reg, would you like a trip o' the sea to Mull?" Jimmy asked with the wonderful friendly tone that they were soon learning was so common with the locals.

"I'd love to" replied Reg. He was fascinated and accepted Jimmy's invitation to go across on the short journey to the neighbouring island.

Phyllis was more than happy to stay behind with Joyce and enjoy the casual conversation. Jimmy was the third generation to operate this ferry which had been in service for 70 years. From April to September it took visitors across to the island, renowned for the variety of wildlife and, in particular, the iconic White Tailed Sea Eagles. On a Wednesday there was also a special ferry sailing to another small island off Mull. This island was called Ulva.

The ferry was only a small boat able to take a maximum of six cars or just a few small trucks. Although it took vehicles to Tobermory the island of Ulva was for pedestrians only. The only means of transport for the few residents on Ulva, now less than 20, were quad bikes. The approach to Ulva was only suitable for smaller vessels, so Jimmy had an arrangement with a fellow skipper, at Tobermory, to take any passengers, on the last part of their journey, to link up with his return ferry crossings.

The trip to Tobermory was still used by local people for visiting friends and also by Jimmy himself who did a good trade in collecting supplies for the neighbours as an alternative to the lengthy round trip to the mainland. Angus also used Jimmy's ferry to send his lobsters to market. Reg delighted in being given a tour of the ferry, the engine room and even the ships log, which he noted made detailed references to every crossing made, including numbers and types of tickets issued. Jimmy informed Reg that 'Ulva' in Old Norse, means 'wolf island', although, these days, whilst it is famous for the wildlife and rare fauna, there are fortunately no wolves to be found.

The two-way crossing and their ensuing conversation took over two hours and when they returned they found Phyllis being shown Joyce's expertise in dressing a freshly caught crab which she insisted that they took home with them for their tea. They gladly took with them a number of leaflets pertaining to both the ferry timings and the attractions to be found on both Mull and Ulva. Phyllis would make sure that both the ferry and the boathouse restaurant would be recommended to their visitors and they bade their farewells, already promising to be regular visitors themselves.

Other visits included a stop at the nearby village inn The Dobhran where they enjoyed a lovely evening meal of Aberdeen Angus beef and once again introduced themselves to the owner, his wife and several of the locals. Reg had pronounced it as Dob-ran but soon learnt that the Gaelic pronunciation was actually doe-ran with the 'b' being silent.

They made a particular point of finding the Ardnamurchan Point lighthouse, which took them initially away from the shore. It didn't matter though because the scenery and the eventual views from the lighthouse were spectacular and well worth seeking out. The lighthouse tea room was not open until Easter but, according to Meg, the cakes were particularly recommended.

They had also been to the mainland to purchase two new freezers and a display fridge which would stay in reception. They had waited in on the expected delivery date and had anticipated that the delivery van might have trouble finding them. They had no postcode to pinpoint an exact location for any satnav but Reg had agreed that he could give Meg's address with further directions from there. The freezers arrived anyway with no trouble and Phyllis made sure that all three were full of all the essential things that they would need.

As promised they were invited to Angus's home for dinner one evening. Angus's wife Elaine was charming as were his three children Donnie 14, Camran 7 and the youngest Paige who was nearly 5. Phyllis chatted to Elaine for ages about her plans for the site and Elaine kindly offered to help with marketing and updating the website. Their home was beautiful with windows offering views all around. It was newly built with the best insulation. There were four bedrooms a spectacular kitchen diner and a large, comfortable lounge. Phyllis worried that she might not be able to fit seven people round her caravan table to return the invite so she promised them a BBQ when the weather improved.

They had prepared detailed directions to the site themselves with Reg giving precise distances between notable landmarks. He particularly warned visitors about the humped-back bridge and not only gave advice regarding how to negotiate it but also offered to meet them there if they cared to ring beforehand. They made sure that all of the clients who had already booked were sent a copy of these directions.

By the end of the month they had taken two more bookings for April and a dozen for the summer months. Not bad for their first season especially considering that according to Touring Haven Holidays, they should expect the bookings to pick up from May onwards.

THE FIRST GUESTS ARRIVE.
AND NORMAN!

AT LAST IT was 1st April, a Saturday. Reg and Phyllis were up at first light anticipating the arrival of their guests. They were expecting Mr and Mrs Bowthorne coming all the way from North Yorkshire. They had booked for a full week and were towing a Sterling Eccles van. They had estimated that they would arrive by 3pm. Later that week, on the Tuesday, another caravan was expected with a gentleman called Mr Philpott and his three dogs. Of course it was always possible that they could also expect some guests who had not pre-booked and it was therefore important to be out and about early.

Phyllis tended her baskets and troughs and Reg positioned the waste bins. He had made numerous signs - for example signs to make sure that guests used the appropriate bins for recyclable items, signs that requested dogs to be kept on a lead when on the site, signs to advise guests that loud music was considered annoying for other guests and signs which pointed the way to areas set aside for ball games. He was particularly proud of the board he had painted showing the correct way to position caravan, awning and car on any pitch. He had turned the board into an easel type structure which stool proudly outside the reception.

Mr and Mrs Bowthorne did not arrive at 3pm as they had expected but Reg and Phyllis had already anticipated that their guests may not have allowed for the extent of the single track roads and the additional time that this entailed. Although they had not taken up Reg's offer to meet him at the bridge he decided to walk there anyway just to check that they had not encountered a problem. The bridge crossed a small burn with a constant yet peaceful sound of running water as it tumbled across the rocks and fallen branches just a few feet below. The bridge and its adjoining silver birch trees were alive with birds, chaffinches, great tits, blue tits and pretty sparrow-sized birds with a glorious yellow tinge. Reg later found out that these were common in Scotland and were actually called siskins. He had, until now, never considered himself to be a 'twitcher'. He had always been too busy to fully appreciate these industrious creatures but, in this tranquil place, he wished that he had brought along his binoculars to see their vibrant colours more clearly.

It was ten past four when the Bowthorne's caravan came in to view. Mr Bowthorne approached the bridge impeccably. Reg was impressed. He wound down his window and Reg gave him a cheerful welcome to Camus and shook his hand. He directed them a hundred yards further on to where they would enter the open gate to the Camus site. They pulled alongside the reception and went up to Phyllis waiting patiently across the desk. Reg soon caught up and was looking forward to seeing their first visiting van sited.

Phyllis welcomed them with a warm smile. Reg also introduced himself and in return the Bowthornes revealed their first names as Mick and Maureen from Brough. Reg quickly assessed them to be in their early 50s. The first topic of conversation was naturally about their journey and how easy it was to find Camus from the directions given. They had found the site easily but had not realised how long it would take from the ferry crossing to cover the last 40 miles. They had only been caravanning for the last two years and had bought their Eccles caravan from a friend to see if they liked it. This was the furthest caravan site they had visited, inspired by various TV programmes about the west coast of Scotland. From what they had seen so far from the car they were not disappointed.

Phyllis completed the necessary paperwork and politely suggested that they might like to return to the reception once they had chosen their pitch. She would put the kettle on anyway in case they would like a cup of tea. Mick was delighted that he could choose his own pitch. Reg showed him the easel indicating how to position his outfit but judging by the way he had negotiated the bridge he didn't feel that he needed to be too prescriptive.

They chose a pitch right at the front pointing the van towards the sea. Reg watched as Mick levelled the van and hooked up to the electric. The caravan was far from new but was in excellent order. As soon as the van was unhitched Reg observed that Mick pulled out a chamois leather and started to clean the caravan windows. He had assumed that they would quickly return to the reception for their cup of tea but Mick took a good ten minutes to clear the flies from the windows. No wonder that their van looked in such good order. Reg even suspected that Mick may also have spent some time in the forces. His attention to detail had been noted. Soon they both returned to Phyllis in the reception and, over a cup of tea, they were given a complete introduction to the site including a site map, details of reception opening hours and lists of items usually stocked not only in the reception but also in Reg's workshop stock room. They had not brought many provisions with them and were pleased to buy some milk and locally baked bread to see them through their first breakfast. Phyllis was particularly proud of her selection of posters and information leaflets which she made them aware of and urged them both to return and make use of the information area once they were settled.

Reg was keen to show them around the site and as they too were happy to stretch their legs, at last so all four went outside together. As they strolled around the site Reg and Phyllis revealed that they were indeed their first guests since they had become wardens at the start of the season. In that respect Mick and Maureen were their guinea pigs and Phyllis was keen for them to be both patient but also honest. Mick and Maureen were making their first visit to Scotland and were asking so many questions in their excitement to plan their week. They stopped at various points, partly to admire the views and partly to see each of the facilities to which Reg was proudly introducing them. He showed them the newly refurbished toilet block assuring them that the water would be nice and hot and that the block itself was heated all day. He had only set out bins in two locations but would be glad to place more if required. It was important to tell them that the electricity supply was only 8 amps and that if they were to use too many appliances at once it might trip out. If this were to happen they should tell Reg who could then reset the MCB.

Soon they approached the steading which, although not used by the visitors and therefore need not feature in his tour Reg couldn't resist - telling them about its history and the work he was intending to do to finish the restoration. They were fascinated and Reg promised to show them the old Fordson during their stay.

Looking out across the bay Mick and Maureen couldn't believe the spectacular views that stretched out in every direction. The boathouse was still in its semi-derelict state as Reg had not had time to attend to it during these early weeks. The old lobster pots and tangled nets were still lying along the beach but somehow it added character to the shoreline. Maureen was becoming increasingly enthusiastic as the tour went on.

"I love to paint" she said "and I'm already seeing so many possible subjects that I doubt I will want to leave Camus at all!"

The tour and ensuing conversation lasted over an hour before Mick and Maureen returned to their van to finish settling in. The reception hours normally ended at six but Reg and Phyllis they told their guests to pop back to their warden pitch if they thought of anything else they needed.

"Oh, by the way" Mick asked "Where can I get a paper in the morning?"

They had dreaded being asked that question as they had not managed to source paper deliveries to the site.

"I'm really sorry" replied Reg "the nearest place is the local village which is almost 10 miles away. I will gladly give you directions in the morning."

He was dreading the first negative response from Mick but it didn't come: instead Mick simply chuckled.

"Well they say that no news is good news so I suppose that bodes well for the holiday."

Reg and Phyllis returned to their van and reflected on their first guests and on their own performance in making them welcome. All seemed to go well so far but when they had more visitors they might have to try again to organise paper deliveries. The first bread delivery had started that very day - three freshly baked loaves and six rolls as a first order with a promise of more which Phyllis would phone through each week.

Reg was up bright and early the next morning being sure to take his shower to check the water temperature. It was perhaps a bit too hot so he went to the controls to make sure it was just right. Phyllis was also ready to man the reception in case their guests needed anything.

Mick was up by 8am and could be seen enjoying the morning air and once again wiping the dew from the caravan windows with his chamois. He had also unloaded all the poles and holdall bags which suggested that he had an awning to erect. There was a fair breeze blowing, not unusual for the Camus site. It would be interesting to see how they got on in these seemingly normal conditions. Mick placed the poles on the ground strategically in position and waited for

Maureen to assume her role. Mick was shorter than average and Maureen was even smaller. They therefore both needed to use an additional step to embark on this procedure.

Reg was keen to offer his support.

"Do you think I should offer to help?" Reg asked Phyllis. But Phyllis encouraged him to stay in the reception.

"No dear" she quickly replied, knowing that he would be sure to take over and his offer of help would soon turn in to a military operation with advice quickly resorting to a series of orders which compelled the other parties to comply.

Fortunately, just at that moment, Angus's pick up could be seen along the the coastal road, approaching the site. He always stopped just before Camus to tend his cattle and then regularly called just to say good morning as he was passing. His imminent arrival allowed Mick and Maureen the chance to erect their awning in their own way. It was a stressful operation even in calm conditions but the breeze was adding to their difficulty. The canvass was blowing uncontrollably like a sail. Mick and Maureen were beginning to argue and blame each other when the poles crashed to the ground.

"You need to secure the guide ropes!" shouted Maureen precariously from her step.

"Thank you for your helpful observation" replied Mick sarcastically as he hurried to get his awning pegs from the holdall. The pegs he had were more suited to softer ground and several broke as he tried to hammer them in to the hard ground.

"Hurry up! My arms are hurting" urged Maureen.

At that moment a sudden gust pulled her from the step and sent the awning flapping once again. Eventually they managed to tie down all the guide ropes but it had taken them an hour and the whole operation had meant that what should have been a memorable and relaxing first breakfast had now descended into tea and toast being taken separately, Maureen in the caravan and Mick at the picnic table under the awning.

After breakfast Mick came to the reception to ask whether Reg had any awning pegs for sale as he feared that if the wind picked up those that he had secured may not hold. Not only did Reg have a supply of the steel screw- in pegs which he had bought for this exact eventuality but he also was only too pleased to offer to come and help Mick with his cordless Dewalt adaptor made specifically for fixing such pegs. Reg and Mick returned together which helped break the tension which now clearly existed between the visiting couple. Whilst the men relocated and fixed all the guide ropes, Maureen went to see Phyllis and take advantage of all her interesting leaflets. She had not paid too much attention to Phyllis's beautiful baskets upon their arrival but now she had more opportunity to comment upon the delightful arrangement of colours. She asked if she would be able to paint them. Of course Phyllis was flattered and agreed with the express condition that she was allowed to see the finished painting. She apologised to Maureen for the fact that it would still be several weeks before they filled the containers completely. Back home in Worcestershire they would have been more advanced by now but she still had to buy many of the plants locally and so they were several weeks' growth behind her usual expectations.

Maureen picked up one of each leaflet that was available to help them plan their week. A trip to the Ardnamurchan

Point lighthouse was surely a must as indeed was the ferry trip to Ulva. Today they were simply intending to go for a walk along the shore and explore the immediate area.

"Do you have any leaflets describing walks and footpaths around the site?" asked Maureen.

"No" replied Phyllis "There's no need. You can walk anywhere here. Nobody minds. The walk along the shore goes a fair way in either direction but there are a few places which require scrambling over the rocks so you'd best wear stout shoes."

"Is everything ok for you both so far?"

"Oh yes thank you" replied Maureen "We thought that we might go to the local inn that you mentioned this evening. Do you have their telephone number to book a table?"

Phyllis laughed "You won't need to book a table" she said "but it's just as well to let them know to expect you. I have a few cards that the owner gave us recently, here take one of these." She handed the card to Maureen along with a personal recommendation for the Aberdeen Angus beef.

Reg soon had their awning properly secured with the steel pegs. He had bought several sets which he had put in the shop for guests to buy. Judging by their first visitors, this may prove a popular item along with the use of his cordless Dewalt. However Reg was not keen on lending his tools lest they were broken or at worst not returned. Unless the site became incredibly busy he thought that the best policy would be for him and his drill to be considered a pair!

As soon as Reg had helped secure Mick's awning he retreated to the steading. He had a couple of hours to spare so indulged himself with the old Fordson. He was gradually taking off each part to clean off years of oil, dust, bird and mouse droppings. He heard the familiar sound of Angus's pick up pulling in to the site and the cheery sound of "morning hen" which was Angus's usual greeting for Phyllis. He had called by to tell her that Elaine had almost finished the web site which she was designing for them and was happy to show Phyllis when she was next passing. Once he saw that Reg was stripping down the Fordson, he couldn't resist hanging around a bit longer. He wasn't due to collect his creels until later that afternoon so the two men disappeared in to the steading for a long session. Phyllis was happy that her guests were well settled so decided to pay Elaine a visit straight away. Whilst in the steading Reg once again heard a faint rustle from up in the eaves. He stopped what he was doing and looked up. Although he had now fixed up lighting above the tractor the far end of the steading was still quite dark. He hadn't got round to clearing out the very back, his only excuse being the urge to focus attention on his tractor.

"Did you hear that?" he asked Angus.

"I expect it's the barn owl" replied Angus knowingly. "She lives in here didn't you know?"

Reg stared up and then went to get his torch to see if he could get a better look.

"She comes out in the early evening from the far end and goes hunting. Elaine and I often see her over our fields and I've spotted her many times from my boat." Angus spoke so acceptingly of what was obviously a normal encounter for him.

"I suppose that Phyllis and I haven't noticed as we only look out on this end of the steading. How long has she been here?" Reg asked.

"We've seen her for the last two years but I don't think many live for long. Of course barn owls don't 'hoot'" he said "they make more of a screeching sound." Reg couldn't see anything but would be sure to pay more attention on his evening round.

Mick and Maureen had started their walk by the boathouse. They had packed their rucksack with four of the rolls they had bought from the shop, their binoculars and camera and Maureen's sketch pad. Sensibly they had packed waterproof jackets following Reg's advice but at the moment the weather was fine but breezy. They made slow progress along the beach stopping every few yards to either look out to sea or inspect the shore and the rock pools. They sat for ages eating their lunch and watching the scraggy looking heron a little further along the shore. Whilst they were watching he caught at least five fish, finally spreading his long wings and flying out to sea, his long spindly legs seeming to trail unnecessarily behind. During their walk they didn't see a soul. Various sea birds were all around and in the distance on the hill top near Camus they could see some highland cows. Maureen vowed that she would paint a picture of a highland cow before the week was out.

Phyllis was delighted at the progress Elaine was making with the web site. Reg and Phyllis had taken several photos themselves but Angus and Elaine had a library of pictures covering all the seasons and in addition they had had many years of waiting for the best weather for photo opportunities.

Phyllis had already visited the Tourist Information Centre back on the mainland and found that they were more than happy to promote Camus and include the website through their own links. Of course Touring Haven Holidays featured Camus on their own web site but the pictures they had were old and Phyllis did not consider that it did the site justice.

The photo just taken of the reception complete with colourful hanging baskets was particularly inviting. Elaine had also designed some new brochures which looked so professional but then her marketing experience was evident. Phyllis had agreed that they should print 2000 using money from the budget they had been given. They could then make sure that 200 were sent to each of the five main tourist information offices. A further 500 could be distributed to local pubs, shops etc and the others could be available for Reg and Phyllis to send following telephone enquiries. Meg had also offered to hand them out to her B&B guests. After all it was not as if they were competing for customers but they might pass them on to caravanning friends.

On the Tuesday morning they were expecting Mr Philpott with his three dogs. He was coming from the Borders and expected to arrive by lunch time. It was already 1pm when Reg decided to walk down to the bridge to see if he was in sight. As he descended from the site he could hear a commotion ensuing and the sound of dogs barking. Mr Philpott's outfit was stuck just before the bridge whilst on the hump of the bridge was a highland cow clearly obstructing his passage. Two of the dogs were still in the car but the third, a brown Labrador, was standing facing the cow and attempting to frighten it in to moving away by continually barking and racing around on his own side of the bridge. The cow looked stubborn and unimpressed. Reg called across.

"Hello there do you need some help?"

"Yes please" came the reply "I've been here for ten minutes now and the beast does not seem keen to move on. Is he yours?"

Reg thought for a moment. He had no experience of these cattle and wasn't sure if approaching from the rear was advisable. The beast's horns were rather intimidating being both very long and very sharp. If he were to make it charge across the bridge it could possibly hurt either Mr Philpott or his dog or make a significant dent in his car or caravan.

"No it's not mine" he replied "I expect that it will move off in a little while."

They stood there for what appeared to be ages when the sound of Angus's pick up could be heard approaching from Reg's direction. As he got out of his pick up he started to laugh and gave Reg a hearty slap on the shoulder.

" Well I knew that Tormad would introduce himself at some point" he said continuing to walk onto the bridge at which point he put his hand deep into his pocket pulling out a handful of pellets which immediately encouraged Tormad to turn tail and slowly follow him off the bridge.

Reg felt rather foolish seeing the previously assumed, intimidating beast adopt a slow, docile stroll behind Angus. Mr Philpott hurriedly put his Labrador back in the car and also crossed the bridge to meet them. The three men were amused by the encounter with both Reg and Mr Philpott, who introduced himself as Colin, eager to learn more about Tormad.

Angus explained that Tormad is Gaelic for Norman. He was about nine years old and has always been fascinated by the arrival of a new caravan ever since he was a calf. He rarely misses a new visitor and has learnt that assuming his position on the hump of the bridge affords him the assurance that the people will get out of the car enabling him to get a better look. It is not unusual for him to stay in position for half an hour and has even been known to stick his tongue out whenever there is a photo opportunity. Angus even wondered if it was his version of a smile!

"Was it animal pellets you had in your pocket?" Reg asked Angus.

"Aye" replied Angus "Norman can easily be encouraged to leave his post in pursuit of more food."

Reg now realised what the dustbin full of pellets found in the steading were for. Good job that he had not thrown them away.

NOVICES NEED SUPPORT

COLIN WAS A widower and had been on his own for the last three years since sadly losing his wife to cancer. He had a Bailey Senator Vermont caravan and an awning in which the dogs would sleep. The dogs were a Labrador, a Beagle and a West Highland terrier all well-used to caravan holidays and looking forward to the endless walks which Colin embarked upon.

People who are used to caravan sites will be aware of the polite notice often displayed "Everyone loves your dog on a lead". Reg hoped that Colin would respect this although walking three dogs together on leads was likely to present its own difficulties. Colin also sited his van near to the shore but respectfully maintaining a distance between himself and Mick and Maureen. He filled in his details in the reception and paid for four nights.

Mick and Maureen knew that another caravan had been expected to arrive that day. Colin had taken the dogs for a walk following their car journey but soon returned and acknowledged them with a simple nod of his head. The three dogs seemed, at first, to be quiet and well behaved but that demeanour only existed when Colin was around. As soon as he left his van to go and fetch water, visit the shower block or had the audacity to take a short walk across the site without them they barked incessantly until he returned. Reg could hear this from his own caravan and was concerned for Mick, Maureen and any other guests who might arrive. He thought that he might ignore it whilst Colin got settled in but would have to speak to him if it continued.

That evening Colin took the dogs for a walk. As he descended the slipway by the boathouse all three were determined to head off in different directions along the shore. As predicted the tangled web of leads took some sorting out but it was only necessary on the Camus site. Colin respectfully carried the requisite supply of poop bags with him and made sure that he cleaned up after each dog. Reg was pleased to see this, ensuring that his immaculate site remained untarnished. Hopefully together they could find a solution to the dogs' barking. He waited until Colin was on his way back to the van and made his way towards him with a cheery good evening.

"The dogs don't like it when you go away do they" Reg started with a light-hearted tone.

"No they think I've gone off for a walk without them. Since my wife passed away they seem to worry that I might disappear as well."

Reg could sense that he would have to continue with sensitivity. "We once had neighbours who had the same problem" Reg started. In reality he was making up the story in order to get his point across. "The trouble was that the dog woke us up each morning, which caused friction between us."

"So what did you do?" enquired Colin realising that the conversation was leading to an expectation that he would have to deal with barking.

"I bought the dog a toy chew which he was given each morning before breakfast. It became part of his daily routine which he so looked forward to that it silenced him whilst my neighbour was getting ready. Have you tried anything to distract them when you have to leave the awning?" asked Reg. "I can't say it will work but it's worth a try".

"It's a good idea" replied Colin "but I don't suppose that there's a pet shop around here"

"Only back on the mainland" Reg informed him. "You could try the village shop they stock a bit of everything there or you might find something you could use as a chew if you go beachcombing. There's lots of interesting driftwood which may provide some amusement."

Reg began to feel sorry for Colin who he thought was only in his mid sixties. His wife must have passed away before they had the opportunity to enjoy their early retirement years. He imagined how he would be if he were to lose Phyllis. In spite of her incessant talking she was good company and shared many of the same interests as himself. Now Colin was facing holidays on his own. Reg knew that he had to deal with the barking problem but he didn't want to make Colin feel unwelcome.

"Would it help if I took the dogs down on to the beach whilst you had your morning shower?" asked Reg.

"Yes they would love that thank you. They are happy to go with strangers and I don't take long getting washed. Are you sure that it's not too much trouble?"

"Not at all" replied Reg wondering what he had let himself in for. He did not think that dog walking would become a regular part of his duties. Hopefully the site would become busier but, at the moment, he was happy to offer Colin his support.

Mick and Maureen were out each day exploring the local area. On the Wednesday they took Jimmy's ferry to Ulva. They returned shortly after 6pm and were keen to tell Phyllis all about it. They had walked, from the pier, through quiet, peaceful glens as far as the ruined township of Ormaig. Maureen was particularly moved by the stories of the clearances and saddened by the tumbled down croft houses, once so busy but now without any sign of life. The ruined houses had, sadly, not been restored but she had found evidence of an old mill and a crofters stove. The island apparently had a population of over 600 at the beginning of the nineteenth century. The township had finally been abandoned following a collapse of the island's economy due to a decline of the kelp market coupled with the further bitter blow brought about by the potato famine. There was also a memorial at Ormaig, celebrating the enduring link of this place to the Clan MacQuarrie. Visitor books at the pier indicated that MacQuarries, from around the globe, still visit the island from time to time

Maureen had made a sketch of the Thomas Telford church found on Ulva. The Church and Manse were built in 1827 but the building was now in a poor state of repair. The last minister left in 1929 and the church no longer holds regular services. She had, of course, taken photos to be sure that she could capture the colours as she fully intended to paint it at some later point. Already she had a long list of subjects including Phyllis's baskets, the boathouse and shore, the church and of course Norman. Mick intended to take in the Ardnamurchan Point lighthouse and all along the coast which would surely afford further inspiration. Whist at the ferry, Maureen had met Joyce and they had had some beautiful fresh oysters followed by home-made cake. For their supper, Joyce had made them her speciality of fresh crab.

It was the next day, when Phyllis was tending her baskets that another caravan pulled up to the reception. This was their first chance visitor. A young couple stepped inside asking if they could have a pitch for a few nights. Phyllis was delighted and immediately pulled out the necessary paperwork. They revealed that they had just got married the previous weekend at Gretna and had accepted the offer of her parents' caravan for several days. They couldn't afford a honeymoon abroad but loved to walk and see the wildlife. They hadn't been caravanning before so the whole venture filled them with excitement. They were impressed with Phyllis's posters she had displayed showing pictures of otters, dolphins, seals and sea birds. She told them to pick a pitch after which she and Reg would take them around the site and give them all the local information.

Their names were Mr and Mrs Clarke they revealed, giving each other a hug, but more informally their names were Chris and Melanie.

Chris moved the caravan around the site very cautiously. It was immediately obvious that he was not experienced. Indeed in his excitement he had not noticed Reg's easel indicating how to position the caravan on the pitch. However that assumed that the driver could actually manoeuvre it on to the pitch in the first place!

Phyllis had gone to the steading to inform Reg that new, unexpected guests had arrived. Reg was covered in oil and grease and said that he would be out to welcome them as soon as he fitted the diesel filter and cleaned himself up.

Chris and Melanie had stopped beside a pitch with spectacular views. To make the most of the views, Chris needed to reverse the van so that the front windows faced the sea. The pitch was a little uneven and there was not enough space to simply drive in going forwards. The art of reversing a caravan may seem simple to the experienced caravanner but is a daunting prospect for those who have not done so before. It took a considerable number of attempts before the van was even vaguely on the pitch. Reg came out of the steading and made his way towards them.

"Afternoon folks" was his greeting. The pair were stifling laughter so as not to appear rude.

"As you may have already gathered" giggled Melanie "we're not good at this".

"Well then" replied Reg "It's your lucky day 'cos I'm Reg, your friendly warden here to help where help is needed. First we need to move the van so that you can hook up to the electric. How long is your lead?"

"Not sure" replied Chris.

"Well let's have a look" suggested Reg. It was at least 10 meters, which would reach the nearest hook up. As Chris had already unhitched the van, Reg agreed that moving it manually to a straighter position was a good idea.

"You need to make sure that it's level" advised Reg, showing them the spirit level just inside the front window "We don't want you rolling about inside do we!" Of course Reg hadn't yet heard that this was to be their honeymoon so he failed to see the humour in his statement. Melanie and Chris however laughed uncontrollably.

"I was given a crash course by my father in law" said Chris "and somewhere I've written down pages of instructions. I'd better get it right or I'll be in trouble" he sniggered.

Reg remembered his first caravan experience and the preparations he had undergone before first setting off. He soon realised that these two novices would certainly require considerable help and quite relished the prospect. First he showed them how to hook up to the electric and switch the fridge from battery. Next he took Melanie to the water point and helped her to connect the water container and the waste while Chris raised and lowered each leg to ensure that the van was level. He was still having trouble when Reg and Melanie returned.

"You probably need to use a large flat stone under the offside front" recommended Reg who straight away picked up a suitable rock from the ground. Melanie returned to the shop to get some milk so that she could make a cup of tea for the two men. Being inexperienced, she had only bought some basic provisions with her and was glad of the one loaf which Phyllis still had in the shop.

"Have you brought something with you for dinner?" asked Phyllis.

"No" replied Melanie "I was hoping to pick up something on the way but we didn't pass any shops. Do you have any food for sale?"

"Follow me dear" said Phyllis locking Melanie's hand in the crook of her arm. She led her in to the store containing the second freezer and together they chose a steak and ale pie and some frozen chips. In the shop Melanie picked up a can of beans and a small tub of ice cream.

"I don't suppose you have any bottles of wine do you?" she asked. Phyllis had bought only a small selection of bottles which they could always use themselves if they didn't sell but Melanie chose the Pinot Grigio.

"It's a special evening for us" she giggled "I don't usually drink but it will be nice to celebrate".

They returned from the shop together by which time Reg and Chris had levelled the caravan and all was settled.

"Shall we take you both around the site?" Phyllis asked.

"Only if you have a cup of tea with us first" replied Melanie who went straight inside to put the kettle on. "Chris there isn't any water" she called out.

"Have you switched the pump on" asked Reg.

"What's the pump?" came the reply.

Reg showed them where the switch was and soon the kettle made the characteristic boiling sound. The other three stood outside taking in the sea air. All of a sudden there was a crashing sound coming from inside the van. Melanie had opened up the cupboard to get some cups but they had moved during the journey and had tumbled out all over the floor.

"Are you ok in there?" Phyllis called out. The door opened and Melanie's face appeared once again laughing. "Yes fine, fortunately they're made of melamine so no harm done."

They moved into the van to enjoy their tea and avoid the passing shower but soon the sun was back out so together they took a tour of the site. Reg felt it necessary to point out every detail as they were clearly raw recruits. He showed them where the bins were, the waste water disposal point, the chemical emptying tank and the shower block. He told them about the other guests currently on the site and where his own caravan was should they need any more help when the reception was closed. Having completed the tour, Reg and Phyllis decided that it was time to leave the young lovers alone to get properly settled in. As he left he dared to ask whether they had brought an awning with them, hoping desperately that the answer was no. Fortunately his assumption was correct. For a brief moment Reg had envisaged at least half an hour's work helping Chris to erect an awning for the first time.

For the rest of that week they therefore had five guests on their site. The order for bread deliveries was now increased to five loaves each day and a dozen rolls. So far everyone they had welcomed seemed nice and friendly, no awkward customers to deal with and no complaints. However they had been told by Touring Haven Holidays to expect some difficulties and, after all, it was early days. That evening they had invited Meg to their caravan for dinner. She had been looking forward to it for ages and wasn't expecting any guests herself until the weekend so it was a good opportunity for her to come and see how they were getting on. The three of them were enjoying a pre-dinner glass of wine when Melanie appeared at the door of their van with a troubled look on her face.

"My oven seems to have stopped working" she said "I'm so sorry to disturb you but I thought you might know what the problem is."

"Let me come and take a look" offered Reg. Melanie could smell the dinner cooking away nicely in Phyllis's oven. Her efforts were considerably less controlled. Already she had burnt the chips whist the pie remained only lukewarm. She had so wanted to make this a special evening for Chris and feared that it was all going disastrously wrong. Reg's suspicion was that their gas had run out. He was absolutely right. They didn't have another bottle with them but Reg had some in the store in his workshop. He went back to his van for the keys and soon had their meal on its way again.

"Oh thank you again" they both said "don't know what we would have done without you".

Meg, Phyllis and Reg sat down to a lovely chicken casserole with dumplings. It was great for them to return the favour that Meg had afforded them on their earlier visit. She had brought with her some shortbread she had made earlier that day. As always it was delicious, and went down so well with the after dinner coffee. The conversation included plans they each had for the forthcoming season; progress they had made preparing the site and work that was still required. Oh and of course the weather which, out here, was so influential in attracting the tourists that it merited considerable discussion.

"You do realise that the midges will be back in May" Meg said.

"I've heard about the midges" replied Phyllis "I don't see what we could do about them though. Have you any suggestions?"

"Well I keep bog myrtle under my hat or behind my ear and, of course I wear a midge net over my head when the beasties are at their worst. Some people swear by Avon Skin So Soft but I've found that bog myrtle works best. Joyce and Jimmy bought a 'Midgeater' last summer to protect their visitors but that's only good in a confined area. I'm afraid that here at Camus you'll find it hard to keep them away."

Meg went on to recount the old tales of shepherds who kept bog myrtle under their hats when out tending their flocks and recounted that even Queen Victoria was said to have abandoned a Highland picnic after complaining of being 'half-devoured' by the beasties. Meg collected her bog myrtle from the peaty bog just before the forest behind the village. The land there is fenced by the forestry commission so the myrtle grows without being grazed by the sheep.

"Och tourists make such a fuss" she said dismissively "I've lived here all my life and they haven't managed to chase me away yet. I doubt they ever will."

Nevertheless Phyllis ordered a supply of bog myrtle pure essential oil and the recommended Avon product as well. Reg considered a midge eater but found that they were several hundred pounds so instead he ordered a supply of midge nets for his guests to purchase if needed. Of course he kept one for himself and one for Phyllis. It was always good to advertise your wares!

It was a lovely evening and Meg laughed aloud as Reg recounted the story of Norman and Mr Philpott's dogs.

"Aye I've had to chase him off the bridge many a time" she revealed "I don't carry pellets with me though I just speak firmly "Tar Tormad!" -in other words move Norman." Meg was keen to drive home before complete darkness fell. She bade them farewell and made her way home.

The next morning Reg honoured his promise. As soon as he could see Colin ready to make his way to the shower block he ventured over to take the dogs for a walk. It was a calm and peaceful morning and the dogs were happy to get out of the awning. Colin had attached their leads and they were all raring to go. Buster, the West Highland Terrier, was the liveliest of all and repeatedly sped around the other two tangling up the leads even before Colin could head off. Alfie, the beagle, had already made up his mind to head for the beach while Delboy the Labrador attempted to follow Colin but soon realised that his friends had their sights set in the opposite direction. Reg was keen to reach the beach as soon as possible as he didn't relish clearing up should the dogs foul the site.

On his way he had to pass Chris and Melanie's van. He couldn't fail to notice that the leg which had been placed on the rock for extra height was now resting on the ground resulting in the whole caravan being on a slant. He could hear them moving around inside but it was too early to disturb them. Perhaps the jolt had woken them up! Delboy, Buster and Alfie were eager to be set free from their web of leads which was holding them back. Reg freed all three and set about combing the shore for driftwood or small floats which they could take back to their awning as toys. Reg had once had a dog himself but that was many years ago and he kind of liked renewing the experience once again. He found a great branch for Delboy to carry along; a remnant of an old buoy which he gave to Buster whilst Alfie had found an old piece of fishing net which took his fancy. Returning from the beach all four of them looked like they had enjoyed the experience but Reg couldn't stop them from running onto the site when they saw Colin coming back from his shower. Each dog was sporting the results of the beachcombing expedition taking his new found toys back in to separate corners of the awning.

IT TAKES ALL SORTS!

IT WAS NOW into April and more bookings had been made covering the Easter holidays which were particularly early this year. As the weekend approached, Mick and Maureen were expected to leave but Maureen was so intent on finishing the paintings she had started that Mick cheerfully entered the office and booked a further five nights. They had decided to make their way to Fort William on the mainland to purchase some new brushes and expand Maureen's selection of paint colours so they were expected to be gone for most of the day.

Colin had taken down his awning as he was moving on further north. Delboy, Buster and Alfie each sported the results of their beachcombing with Reg although the objects were showing the evidence of considerable chewing. Colin came in to the reception before he finally pulled away. He shook Reg firmly by the hand indicating his appreciation of his support and friendship.

"I've really enjoyed my stay here" he said approvingly "I do wish you every success as wardens. You have a beautiful site here at Camus one I shall almost certainly return to". They both waved him off and watched as he went out of sight down the road towards the bridge.

Chris and Melanie, the newlyweds, had paid for a full two weeks. Having set themselves up at last they were fearful of repeating the process all over again by moving on elsewhere. They were going to treat each other to a wildlife trip from Mull as a sort of joint wedding present.

"What a lovely idea" said Phyllis "you're sure to see things you can treasure for ever."

The brochures Phyllis had in the information area included boat trips aimed at spotting sea mammals, boat trips to see the puffins on the smaller islands or even guided tours to watch the sea eagles from an RSPB hide. The sea mammal trips were better a little later, from say June onwards, when there was more chance of the plankton being in abundance and hence more chance of minke whales etc. They finally chose the boat trip to the Treshnish Isles to see the puffins. Melanie had always wanted to see them. They were such comical little birds with an abundance of character. The leaflets for the trips virtually guaranteed that visitors would get close to them so, as this combined a sea journey and wildlife, they rang and made a booking for the following Wednesday. That would obviously require a trip on Jimmy's ferry across to Mull so they decided to head off and check out the ferry time and thereby complete the itinerary for that day.

As the weekend arrived, two more caravans were expected - one bringing their first family of five and one with a further couple. This would bring their expected guest numbers to eleven.

The first van, with the couple, had telephoned in advance to take up Reg's offer to meet them at the bridge. It was raining hard so Reg donned his sou'wester and wellies and set off to greet them. Norman had not been put off by the weather though. After all, he did come from what is renowned to be the hardiest breed in the world. He didn't look at his best with the rain dripping from his thick hairy coat and his 'dossan' or fringe, covering his eyes though it clearly didn't prevent him from seeing who was about to arrive.

Reg had brought a small bucket of pellets from the steading which he placed on the grass just on the roadside over the bridge. He could see that the caravan was a twin axle Swift Challenger one of the newest, so far, to come to Camus. Sadly it didn't look its best as the rain soaked roads had left their mark with muddy splatters not only on both sides but also on the front and rear windows. I hope that he also has a chamois thought Reg and he moved up to the driver's window to greet them.

"So glad to see you. You must be relieved to have finally got here."

"We are" they replied.

"Follow me, the Camus site is only just up there." Reg walked on briskly, indicating with an extension of his left arm the entrance to the site. He looked like a job's worth car park marshall. In reality there was no need as the site entrance was obvious.

Phyllis was ready and waiting patiently in the reception. Their guests pulled alongside and quickly ran from their car in to the office. They were a very smart-looking couple, both wearing matching wax jackets and pristine trainers. Phyllis thought that they were probably similar in age to herself and Reg. She welcomed them with a promise that the weather would improve. Already she had learnt that these spells of rain could soon pass. They completed the booking in form. They were Mr and Mrs Henderson from Northumberland and they were staying for a full week. As it was still raining in stair rods, Phyllis gave them a site map and suggested it might be better if they chose a pitch for now and when the rain had stopped she would give them a tour of the site. As they pulled away, the caravan went down two divots which had opened up outside the reception, spurting yet more muddy puddles up the side of the van. Reg quickly realised that he would need to sort out the immediate entrance before too many vans arrived. Tarmac would be the best form of surface alternatively a decent layer of compacted gravel might be adequate. He immediately made himself a note to add it to his still busy task list.

The Hendersons did not chose a front pitch; instead they stayed a little further back, partially sheltered by some gorse bushes and large boulders which seemed to create a natural private pitch. The ground was particularly wet though. Reg and Phyllis hoped that the twin axle van would not get stuck.

The rain continued for a good two hours after the Hendersons had arrived. Apart from unhitching the van and dropping the corner stays they took refuge quietly inside. There's something about caravanning which compels others to watch every activity. Mrs Henderson was clearly arranging everything inside her van. A vase of false flowers in cream and crimson red was placed on the front chest. Phyllis often wondered why people brought so many home comforts with them. It was all extra things to pack and take up space. Mrs Henderson could also be seen making up the fixed bed with what looked like a cream duvet and getting a co-ordinated cream kettle down from the cupboard. When the rain finally stopped they ventured out, putting on clean green wellies, and starting to get everything ready. They had all the top of the range accessories two aqua rolls, a waste master, a wheel clamp and two sparkling foldaway bikes which they stood up outside the van. Mr Henderson had corner footpads for each caravan leg which he put in place now that the rain had stopped. He was also clearly checking the TV reception judging by the movement of the on board aerial. Reception at Camus was not bad as they were right on the coast and the signal was therefore not blocked by mountains. Phyllis decided to leave them to their own devices. The site map was a clear enough indicator of each of the facilities and whilst she had enjoyed the opportunity to chat to every guest when taking them round the site, she had come to realise that a tour was not exactly necessary. Unlike their previous guests, Mr and Mrs Henderson must have come well prepared. They didn't even return to the shop for bread or milk which was a real pity as Phyllis had increased the bread order yet again. Never mind, she could always make a bread pudding for dessert and perhaps they could have toast for breakfast so as not to waste anything.

By late afternoon Mick and Maureen had returned. Mick's first job was to get out his chamois and dry off every part of his van. He always believed in making the most of the pure water. If it was dried off quickly it left no smears or streaks and using the natural rainfall ensured that the van was kept clean without the necessity to fill a bucket. Maureen came to see Phyllis in the reception to show her what she had bought and to check that she had sufficient colours to paint her baskets. They had spent most of the day in Fort William and had taken a stroll along the Caledonian Canal. It hadn't rained at all until they were on their way back and they were quite surprised to see how much rain had fallen at Camus.

"It's not unusual apparently" said Phyllis "In Scotland it can rain in one glen but be perfectly dry in the next. We have no protection when it's coming from the west though."

"You must be expecting more guests" announced Maureen knowingly.

"Yes, how did you know?" Phyllis asked quizzically.

"Because Norman is waiting on the bridge" laughed Maureen "We came back the other way today so we didn't need to move him!"

As she returned to her van, she passed the Hendersons and stopped for a chat. The lovely thing about folk setting up on a site means that conversation soon flows quite naturally. Phyllis could see them from her window and felt quite excluded. She thought that she would go and check whether the new arrivals needed anything before she was due to close the reception for the day.

Mrs Henderson had introduced herself and her husband as Pat and Paul. Maureen was impressed by their new van and quickly accepted the offer, on behalf of Mick and herself, of a tour round although it was clearly indicated by the Hendersons own slippers placed strategically just inside the door that they too would be expected to take off their shoes. Maureen was a regular reader of each month's caravan magazine and was always amazed by the improvements displayed in full glossy colour in all the adverts which notably seemed to take up every other page. However she hadn't previously been given the opportunity to step inside one. The Hendersons were clearly keen to show off their new toy and point out all its features.

"Wow" gasped Maureen. "It makes our van look very dated now doesn't it Mick."

"We only picked this up from the dealer a few weeks ago" revealed Paul "We got a very good deal and decided to treat ourselves. I'm afraid that it doesn't look at its best at the moment. The journey has taken its toll. I noticed that you were doing the sensible thing chamoising yours just now. I think I'll do the same before it all dries off."

"Where are you from?" enquired Mick.

"We come from Wooler in Northumberland" said Paul "The journey wasn't too bad apart from the rain but then you expect that when you come to Scotland" he laughed.

"How long are you staying?" asked Maureen politely.

"We're here for a week. We came here ……. was it four or five years ago?" Pat asked Paul "Well anyway it doesn't matter. We loved it so much then that we decided to come back. I see the wardens are new though".

"Yes" agreed Maureen "They seem very nice though and very helpful. We only booked for a week but like you we've been so impressed that we've just booked another five nights."

Phyllis had not been able to miss out on the conversation that was clearly going well. She appeared outside the Henderson's van and politely tapped on the door.

"Sorry to interrupt" she said, although in reality she wasn't a bit sorry. She had fully intended to gate crash the party! "I wondered if you need anything before I shut the shop? My what a lovely van" she said as she peeped her head inside secretly hoping to be asked in.

"I think we are ok for this evening thank you" Pat replied.

"Let me know if you want a tour of the site, it's no trouble" Phyllis offered.

"We checked out the site map while it was raining so I think we'll be fine thank you" replied Paul.

"You can always pop over and ask us if you need anything" suggested Maureen.

Phyllis got the distinct impression that she was not needed and was about to walk away when Paul asked, "Does Jimmy still operate the ferry?"

Well, Phyllis couldn't have been given a better cue

"Yes indeed he does. Do I assume that you've been here before?" Phyllis was at last included in the conversation. She was keen to hear about previous visits only hoping that Camus was going to fare up well to any return guests' expectations.

"We were here …… was it four or five years ago?" repeated Pat.

"I think 5 years ago" answered Paul "I understand that you have recently taken over as wardens."

"Yes indeed. I'm Phyllis and my husband is Reg. We hope that everything will be to your liking but if not don't hesitate to let us know. If we are not in the reception, you can always call at our van. We're here to help. Do you know Jimmy then?" enquired Phyllis.

"Not really" replied Paul "I just remember him from all those years ago".

"We're took his ferry to Ulva on Wednesday" interrupted Maureen. "The island is steeped in history and there are old crofting townships to explore. I loved it. It's well worth a visit."

"We went there when we were here before. Perhaps, this time we'll go to Mull to see the Sea Eagles." said Paul. "I'm glad to see that the cow is still around".

"Aye" said Phyllis. "Listen to me" she chuckled "I'm already sounding like a local and I've only been here for six weeks! He's called Norman and the bridge is his regular spot for checking out new arrivals. He belongs to Angus the farmer up the road. Angus calls in from time to time so you may get to see him. He drives a pick up and often stops by."

Maureen excused herself so that she could return to her van and start the dinner. She and Mick had brought back ample provisions from their trip in to town. Mick was particularly looking forward to the bottle of 10 year old malt he had brought back.

"I'm looking forward to a dram or two so they say up here" he laughed.

"Well if you want any help with that just give me a call" replied Paul glancing quickly in Pat's direction in anticipation of a disapproving look. Mick and Maureen left leaving Phyllis still deep in conversation with Pat. It was difficult to judge who could talk the most, Phyllis or Pat. Perhaps Paul's jest of sharing a dram with Mick might not be such a bad idea after all.

Coincidentally Chris and Melanie had been to see Jimmy to check out the ferry in preparation for their boat trip on Wednesday. They needed to catch the return crossing to Mull which departed at 8.30 in the morning and returned at 6:00 in the evening. A minibus would collect them from the ferry and take them to where their boat departs on Mull. It would be a long memorable day according to Jimmy and they had therefore returned even more excited than they were before. They made their way to their van, now obviously more familiar with the daily routine of a caravan site than they were in the beginning. They had bought a few provisions from the village store and looked forward to a quiet evening in, as if any evening at Camus was anything apart from quiet. They walked passed the Hendersons van which Paul was busy cleaning and acknowledged him with the usual "hello". Being young and unfamiliar with the usual normality of stopping to engage other caravanners in conversation, they quickly moved on towards their own van. From the smart, orderly appearance of Paul they had assumed that he was not likely to be interested in anything frivolous that they might be inclined to say.

The next day a large motor home approached the bridge. It had a particularly long wheelbase which together with the usual obstruction of Norman caused the driver to stop and consider how he might safely proceed. As usual Reg was on duty and heard the sound of voices as he was emptying the bins on the site. This was obviously the expected Cole family. Sue, the mother, Graham and the three children all got out considering the predicament. Two of the children were teenagers, two girls whilst the youngest was a boy who was obviously pre-school age. Sue picked up the little boy who was otherwise intent on running straight up to Norman. The teenager's contemptuous faces soon changed to a smile for the first time since they stopped for a burger at the service station nearly four hours ago.

"You need to get him to move" suggested one of the girls.

"Well that's obvious" rebuffed the other.

"Don't start!" snapped Sue.

"Mummy can I stroke him?" asked the little boy as he wriggled from her arms

"No" said Sue "He's got big horns which could hurt you".

Graham was contemplating what he should do, being the only man in the family, when Reg appeared on his way down the road.

"Good day" he called out "I'm Reg the warden. He won't hurt you I'll get him to move on".

Using his bucket of pellets Reg soon diverted Norman's attention and he moved aside. Reg approached Graham extending his hand for the usual greeting.

"My, that's a large vehicle" he quickly assessed "We will need to take the bridge very carefully. Would your wife and the children like to walk up to the site it's only just across the way. My wife Phyllis is expecting you." The teenagers' smiles soon returned to a snarl at the prospect of walking even a short distance. The little boy was, on the other hand, full of excitement as he, at last, had the opportunity to run free. As

Reg had suggested they proceeded to cross the bridge. Reg and Graham were therefore left in peace to consider the best way for the motor home to cross without grounding out. Reg took charge by giving Graham specific instruction, starting with reverse so as to line himself up for the approach. He used his arms to get Graham to move forward, left, right and raised the palm of his hand to give the instruction to stop. Their first attempt resulted in the vehicle only just crossing the hump when Reg banged the windscreen and shouted "Stop!" He could see that the axle would not clear the bridge. He doubted that a different angle of approach would make much difference. He thought for a moment and told Graham that he had some sturdy planks in his shed which might help. The two men therefore left the van and followed the rest of the family back to the site.

"The trouble is that I'm blocking the road" said Graham "Should I reverse it back while we are away?"

"No, I shouldn't worry" replied Reg "You'd still be blocking the road and no-one else is likely to come along." Reg took Graham in to the corrugated shed and went straight to his supply of wooden planks neatly stacked against the wall.

"We probably need about four" he said "they're heavy so we'll take them in my jeep". Reg could already visualise his plan. The planks would be laid on the opposite side of the hump thereby evening out the angle, extending the downside of the slope and consequently prevent the grounding. Together they executed the manoeuvre successfully. Twenty minutes later the motor home pulled onto the site.

Phyllis had been meeting the rest of the family in the reception. The two girls were 14 and 16 and their names were Charlotte and Natalie. It was hard, even for Phyllis to engage them in conversation.

"Have you been to Scotland before?" she asked.

"No" was the single word response.

"What do you intend to do whilst you're here" she tried again.

"Don't know" replied Charlotte the eldest.

The little boy was introduced as Max. His excitement was boundless. "I'm going to ride my scooter, fly my kite, catch fish and sail my boat" he said excitedly as he ran around the office.

"Well you're going to have a lovely time then" Phyllis said, smiling at Sue. She tried to extend the smile to the two girls but they had already walked back outside as their dad pulled up.

"You can take any pitch" advised Phyllis "but you'll probably be better off with one of these two" she indicated by placing two crosses on the site plan. "They are both longer pitches but both have clear views of the sea". Max strained on his toes trying hard to see the plan on the top of the counter.

"Get down Max" instructed Sue "Shall we come back to tell you which one we choose?"

"Oh no, don't worry" replied Phyllis "I'll be able to see you from here". Once again Max ran out of reception with Sue in hot pursuit. She walked on in front of Graham indicating where to go. Charlotte and Natalie had crawled back in to the motor home to join their dad. Phyllis could see from their faces that the excitement was clearly not evident throughout the family. She remembered the sulky teenage years of her own daughter, now grown up, and felt a deep sympathy for Graham and Sue.

That evening Camus was a hive of activity. It was still bright and sunny and almost no wind at all. Pat and Paul had taken their portable BBQ from the hold and Paul had spotted a good area behind the rocks on his pitch. Pat was busy preparing the kebabs. Her large fridge held all the necessary ingredients including peppers, chicken, beef and tomatoes. Maureen stopped by and was immediately invited by Pat for both her and Mick to join them. Maureen had bought sausages in the town planning to have a BBQ herself on the first suitable evening. Paul had already erected his brand new Isabella awning earlier that day. The colour was totally in keeping with the van itself and Pat had prepared the dining table with the finest cream china and proper glasses. Maureen agreed to bring the wine and of course Mick thought that another dram of his malt might not go amiss once they had eaten.

Chris and Melanie had moved their picnic chairs outside too. Although they had no awning to sit under, it was one of those evenings when one was not necessary.

The Coles could be seen setting up. They had a pull-out awning to the side and started to unload the contents of their trailer. The two girls had gone down to the beach, ear pieces in place listening to their iPods. Such a shame thought Phyllis. If only they could take the same pleasure in listening to the lapping of the waves on the shore, the sound of oyster catchers, redshanks and ringed plovers. Their attachment to their iPods meant that they could not hear Sue as she called them back to take care of Max, who was already running around with his kite dragging along the ground becoming tangled in everything that Graham was unpacking. Sue went down to the beach to fetch them.

"Now c'mon girls your dad has had a long drive and surely it's not too much to ask for you to participate" she said sharply.

"What do you want me to do?" asked Natalie most ungraciously.

"Anything would be useful" retorted Sue "take those earphones out for a start. Charlotte you can take Max down to the beach but keep your eye on him. Natalie you can help by making your father and me a cup of tea. Oh by the way Max needs to be shown where the toilet block is."

The girls reluctantly followed their instructions, leaving Graham and Sue to sort everything out. As the trailer was unpacked, out came five pairs of wellies in differing sizes, backpacks, Max's scooter, an inflatable dinghy and even a small outboard motor. There were also a number of fishing rods, a large tackle box and a landing net. Several toys - designed clearly for Max's entertainment including a football, a cricket bat and swing ball were also laid out on the ground.

Sue rigged up the water supply and took the picnic chairs from the hold placing them under the extended canopy. She had put up the folding picnic table outside and brought out drinks and crisps to keep the troop going until dinner time. Natalie brought the tea out to her parents.

"Have you checked the telly out yet" she asked "only Hollyoaks will be on soon."

"No, can't you see I've been a bit busy" snapped Graham. "We've only just got here and you're already thinking about watching telly. I despair!" he said turning his back on her.

"Thanks for the tea Natalie" she said sarcastically, to herself, as she went off to find her two siblings.

"Come and sit down and have your tea dear" encouraged Sue "It seems really nice here doesn't it?"

At last Graham stopped what he was doing and took a good look out to sea. The small islands offshore looked spectacular, particularly given the turquoise hue of the sea exaggerated by the blue sky.

"What a good time to arrive" he noted "the sea looks so calm. I hope it stays like that when we take the dinghy out."

"Shush don't speak too soon" urged Sue "or it might change. I was planning to do something quick for dinner perhaps lasagne and garlic bread I've brought with us".

"Lovely" replied Graham, who was feeling rather peckish after his long drive.

"Cor, smell that BBQ" he said as Paul's first sausages were starting to waft across the site.

Pat, Paul, Mick and Maureen were clearly enjoying their meal and the pleasure of each other's company. The conversation between them flowed easily through their shared passion for walking and caravanning. Somehow BBQs always encourage you to eat more than you would for an average meal. Everyone compelled to being served with a least one, if not two, of every type of meat together with at least one roll and a full complement of the salad dishes which Pat had laid out across the table.

"Does anyone fancy a stroll along the shore to help the dinner go down?" enquired Maureen.

"Good idea" agreed Pat "it's such a lovely evening". The ladies walked on ahead with the men following a short distance behind. As they descended the slipway, Pat spotted something dart across the tarmac and quickly disappear into the sea.

"Did you just see that?" she asked Maureen.

"I caught something out the corner of my eye" she replied "but I don't know what it was". They turned around to see if the men had noticed but they were obviously engrossed in manly conversation not even aware that the ladies had stopped.

"Something just ran across the slipway" declared Pat "It disappeared into the water".

"Where" asked Paul, bringing his binoculars up to take a better look. He looked out across the water but couldn't see anything above the surface. "Stay still but remain quiet" he requested "it might come back". All four stayed exactly where they were and Mick joined Paul although his binoculars were obviously not as expensive or as strong as Paul's. Mick was panning round just offshore, inspecting the kelp that was calmly bobbing across the gentle waves.

"Look over there" he pointed and whispered to Paul who immediately re-directed his bins.

"I think it's an otter" said Paul with some excitement in his voice. The otter had obviously just surfaced having caught a crab which he was preparing to eat whilst floating calmly on his back. Paul's bins could make out every detail of the catch whilst Mick could only see that the otter was eating something.

"Here ladies take a look but try not to move" Paul said, carefully passing his bins to Pat whilst Mick offered his to Maureen.

"Ah look" they both said simultaneously.

"I've never seen a wild one before" said Pat.

"Me neither" added Maureen "Mind you, it said on some of the leaflets I got from the office that otters could be found around here." At that moment Max ran down the slipway with Charlotte in hot pursuit. The otter dived back down and it seemed unlikely now that it would appear again.

"Come on Max" called out Charlotte, "It's time for dinner" although she knew that her chance of getting an excited Max back to the motor home without a tantrum was remote.

"Evening" said Pat to Charlotte.

"You must be with the new arrivals today".

"Yeah" came the one word response as she chased her brother down to the water's edge and dragged him, screaming, by the hood of his sweatshirt back up the slipway.

The adults walked on a little further before returning to the awning for an evening of coffee and after dinner drinks.

"A very special end to another lovely day" said Maureen, full of contentment as she reclined in Pat's exceptionally comfy chair.

REG'S NIGHTMARE

WHEN MONDAY CAME, Reg's first task was to check with Touring Haven Holiday offices whether they could arrange for an emergency repair to the site entrance. He was informed that requests for scheduled repairs should have been received by 1st March and that emergency repairs were expected to be undertaken by the wardens themselves. If the estimated amount was less than £200 it should be met from the budget they had been allocated. If, on the other hand, it was likely to cost more he should seek prior approval from the office.

Reg had already worked out that he needed several wheelbarrow loads of gravel or hard core to first fill the holes and, say, six bags of cold tarmac, which he knew he could get delivered from Travis Perkins in Fort William. He asked Phyllis to place the order for the next day's delivery. He looked around the site to see whether there were any old bricks that he could break up to act as hard core. He had absolutely no intention of using any of the ancient rocks which had dislodged from the steading. Those stones and rocks had been carefully chosen and carried by men with their bare hands. They had built the steading with love and passion, probably carrying each stone some distance from the surrounding area, Reg respected that. To shatter not just their physical appearance but also their immense historical value just to fill a hole was not worthy of consideration. Instead he walked around the site, poking the overgrown bushes and nettle beds with a long stick in the hope that he might find something he could use. Eventually he found a few broken bricks deep amongst some brambles. Having donned his heavy duty gloves, he managed to extract them from their sunken retreats but there was barely one wheelbarrow full. He then remembered that Angus still had some building rubble in the corner of his field left over from the building of his house.

The following day the weather forecast was for rain to arrive by late afternoon so Reg was keen to make good progress. First he would need to break up the rubble and fill the holes before laying the tarmac on top. He jumped into his jeep to ask Angus whether he could use some of his rubble. With any luck Angus might offer to come and lend a hand which would guarantee that it would be finished before the rain was due. However, when he arrived, Elaine and the two youngest children, Paige and Camran, were already in the car and Angus was just coming out of the house. Reg had never seen him looking so smart in a new pair of jeans and a clean denim shirt.

"Hi Reg" the children called out from the open windows.

"Mornin where are you all off to?" he replied.

"We're going to visit Gran in Oban and she's made us her best fruit scones" they said climbing across each other to lean out of the window.

"Did you want something?" asked Angus "We'll nae be back until later this evening".

"I just wondered whether I could take some of your old bricks and hard core to repair the road entrance?" asked Reg.

"Aye, nae problem take what you want. See you later" Angus got into his car and off they all went with the children frantically waving goodbye.

It took Reg all morning the load up the jeep with enough rubble. After lunch he took his sledgehammer from the shed to crush the larger pieces. Fortunately no new visitors were expected to arrive that day and anyway Reg had placed cones by each pothole to mark the spot. This meant that the guests, when driving off the site, needed to weave about to avoid displacing them. Most of the guests were indeed making the best of the day out exploring the area. Mick and Maureen were the only couple to have stayed on site.

The fine weather continued into the afternoon. Maureen was enjoying the sunshine and was nearing completion of her painting of the baskets. She had expanded the picture to include the reception building itself, adorned with the baskets hanging from the brackets put up by Reg and also the long troughs fixed to the fence. Of course, Phyllis had removed any withered or faded blooms first. Mick had gone for a stroll along the shore, wondering whether he might be lucky enough to see the otter once more. However, the sound of Reg hammering somewhat spoilt the usual serenity of the site and it seemed unlikely that the otter would return today.

When Reg finally filled the last hole it was already late afternoon and the dark clouds were approaching menacingly from the west. The Coles arrived back from their explorations. Natalie and Charlotte both headed straight for the shower block intent on washing their hair which had been somewhat ravaged by the sea breeze. It seemed that all their guests had spotted the incoming rain as there was a sudden return of vehicles carefully negotiating their way around the cones. Pat and Paul returned from their cycling trip just in time. The forecast had not predicted rain until early evening but the breeze had picked up and Reg feared that it would arrive sooner than he thought. Although Pat was a little unsteady on her folding bike the roads here were so quiet and ideal for nervous riders. They would ride off, each day, often returning with Pat on foot. The advancement in years forced her to turn tail after just a few miles.

Reg had successfully covered the first of the pot holes with tarmac when the rain started. He had been determined to get them all finished before the rain came in earnest, which risked washing away all the loose gravel and rubble. He therefore hastily covered the others with anything he could find, for example spare notice boards or upturned bins but the uneven surface meant that despite all his efforts, small trickles quickly became targeted rivers.

Reg's calm collected manner was beginning to falter when, as if to add to his predicament, Paul appeared in reception to inform Phyllis that there was no hot water in the shower block. She called Reg in and he quickly re-assigned his priority to the task which more imminently threatened the comfort of his guests.

He went first to the main fuse box in the boiler room and could see that the rain now kicked up by the strengthening breeze had forced its way in through the roof and was seen dripping from the electrical switch near to the boiler. Simply changing the fuse was not an option. Firstly he needed to make a deflector the prevent more rain being blown in through the eaves and then it would need time to dry out before it would be safe to switch the water heater back on. He went back outside to take the required measurements and then locked himself away in his shed and immediately started to make a deflector from the scrap metal he had set aside in his store. Usually Reg relished the opportunity to fix anything. He would spend hours meticulously cutting each piece making sure that not only was it functional but also that it looked professional. His years of training in the army had taught him that if a thing's worth doing it's worth doing well. However today time was of the essence not only because his guests might expect a hot shower before dinner but also because he needed to tend to his pot holes which by now were probably full, once again, with water. It took Reg a while to make the required piece and then scale the roof to rivet it in place covering the area through which the water was penetrating. As it was still raining hard, Reg's blue boiler suit was soaked through.

He was about to ask Phyllis to use the 'Closed for Cleaning' sign to stop their guests from entering the shower block when Pat appeared to let Phyllis know that one of the ladies' toilets was overflowing across the floor. Reg couldn't believe it - every malfunction suddenly seemed to be coming at once.

The fuse box was left to dry out and Phyllis had been dispatched to check out the ladies' toilets. When she went inside she was confronted by one cubicle where water had spilled from the toilet and spread out across much of the floor. A quick tentative inspection looked as though it was blocked. She returned to give Reg a full update. He immediately went in to the ladies' to see what needed to be done. He had always expected that these unpleasant jobs would require attention one day but somehow he found it particularly uncomfortable to be faced with such problems in the ladies' toilets! The toilet had been blocked by a considerable deposit which had then been topped up by endless quantities of toilet paper. Successive attempts to flush by the offender had not cleared the blockage but had simply resulted in the disastrous flood. Phyllis assured him that it was not Pat as she had merely reported the incident. Reg had dealt with similar problems, in the past, and quickly assessed that a plunger and rod would be required so he sped off once again to his shed, issuing instructions to Phyllis to fetch her mop and bucket. He soon returned and dealt with the source of the problem but the ladies' wash area now needed a thorough clean. Phyllis realised that this was her role, leaving Reg to return to the boiler room.

He couldn't even contemplate what had happened to the site entrance. What a disastrous sequence of events he thought. He couldn't risk firing up the boiler again until he was certain that the fuse box was completely dry. His deflector seemed to be working though for although it was still raining hard no more water was being blown in. It took Phyllis a good hour to clean the ladies' toilet block. She had to clean the toilets, mop and then scrub the floor, disinfect the whole area and finally place a new air freshener to ensure that the ladies' wash room was returned to a more pleasant state.

Later that evening they returned to their van. The rain had stopped but the light was now fading. Camus was awash with surface water but hopefully by morning everything would return to normal. Reg lifted a few of his temporary pothole covers. He could see that most were now full of water. This would now significantly delay the opportunity to surface them with the cold tarmac until they had completely dried out. What Reg needed was a few dry, sunny days but in the meantime the obstacle course of bollards would have to remain. No new arrivals were expected for the next two days which was fortunate because, whilst the cars could negotiate around them, a caravan in tow would not be so easy to manoeuvre. Reg was still trying to work out who must have been responsible for blocking the toilet. It wasn't Pat - and Maureen would surely have quietly owned up to Phyllis as they had such a good rapport. Any of the adults would surely have reported the problem in spite of their embarrassment so Reg deduced that one of the young girls must have been the culprit. They had clearly been in the block shortly before to wash their hair.

"What does it matter" sighed Phyllis who was not particularly concerned with assigning blame. "It's all sorted now dear. Can we please change the conversation?"

Later that evening Reg returned to check the boiler room. The fuse box looked dry enough so he reset the boiler switch and it fired up. He breathed a sigh of relief realising that hot showers would be restored in the morning.

As Reg had hoped, the next few days were dry and sunny. They could hear Max's excited voice as Graham was inflating the dinghy. He called in to the reception to check with Reg whether it was OK for him to set off from the slipway.

"Not a problem" said Reg. "Where are you intending to go?"

"Oh just taking Max out for a little tour around" he said. "I've promised him that we'll do some fishing, he's so excited"

"I can tell" laughed Reg. "Phyllis and I could hear him across the site. You be careful though. I'm no sailor but I understand that the currents around these islands can be stronger than you think".

"That's OK" said Graham confidently "I've got an outboard so we'll manage".

Sue had bought some of the rolls from the shop to make the boys a picnic. Max came with her and chose his favourite crisps and some sweets and tucked them away in his Handy Manny lunch box.

"I hear you're going out in the boat with your dad" said Phyllis "I wish I could come!"

"You can" replied Max. "We're going to catch some fish and I've got my own net"

"Well I'm afraid I need to stay here in case any more caravans arrive. You have a fun day though."

Sue informed Phyllis that she was taking the girls to Fort William shopping.

"They're hard work" she told Phyllis, "full of hormones and attitude!"

Phyllis recommended a few particular shops and a visit to Neptune's Staircase, the series of lochs at the start of the Caledonian Canal.

"You're sure to see some boats moving through" she said "It's also a good place for a picnic."

"I think I'd rather be staying with the boys" she laughed. "How long will it take to get to Fort William?" she asked.

"Oh you'd better say an hour" Phyllis replied.

"We probably won't be back then until later this afternoon. At least it's a nice day for taking the boat out." She went back to their motor home with Max to make up the rolls for their picnic.

Graham put his own rod and Max's net in to the dinghy and sensibly put on their life jackets. Max jumped into the boat and was immediately told to sit down and sit still. Graham started the outboard and they set out. Sue, Natalie and Charlotte stood on the shore and waved them goodbye before getting in to the car to head off to the shops. The sea was fairly calm but as the dinghy picked up speed it bobbled about across the waves. Max could be heard squealing with excitement until they had rounded the bay. Graham continued out to sea looking for a decent spot to stop and cast his line. He had just gone round the headland when he decided to stop and see what they might catch. Max was, at last, allowed to put his net in the water in the hope that he too might catch a fish. He couldn't yet cast his dad's line but he was allowed to hold the rod which made him feel very important and very grown up. As soon as the outboard was silent, Graham realised that they were drifting a fair way. He could see from the shore line that there was indeed a strong current just as Reg had said: in fact since going round the headland they had completely lost sight of Camus. He wasn't worried though as they still had the shore in sight and he was really enjoying the tranquillity.

Max was getting hungry and keen to explore the contents of his lunch box. He knew that it contained his favourite Starburst sweets which he could have once he'd eaten his roll. Graham was about the sink his teeth in to the home baked roll when there was a tug on his line.

"Hey look Max" he said. "I think we've caught a fish. Let Daddy take the rod for a minute".

Max was happy to hand it over and lent over the side of the dinghy to see what they had caught. When his dad reeled it in, a small fish, about the size of a fish finger, wriggled on the end of the line.

"Let me take him off the hook" said Graham. "Do you want to keep him in your bucket?"

Max quickly put down his lunch box and handed the bucket to his dad who promptly leaned over the side and scooped up some water. Plop! In went the silver fish in to its new cramped enclosure.

"Put it on the floor" he told Max as he re-baited his line.

"I'm gonna call him Nemo" said Max as he leaned over, watching the fish intently.

"When we've had lunch we'll go nearer to the shore so you can catch some more in your net" said Graham.

While they were enjoying lunch there was yet another tug on the line. Graham reeled it in but this time the fish was even smaller so he carefully released it from the hook and threw it back in. By now he realised that he had drifted a fair distance round the headland and, in addition, was now further from the shore so he thought it was time to start up the outboard and keep his promise to Max to give him the chance to fish with his net. He pulled hard on the cord but the motor simply spluttered. He tried again several times but without success. He realised that he must stay calm so as not to upset Max. He looked all around but other than the odd floating gull or razorbill they were all alone. He had one small oar in the bottom of the dinghy which was really there to help push them off before lowering the motor.

"We're going to row the boat back Max so sit still and be a good boy."

Max was enjoying his packet of Starbursts and was fascinated by watching Nemo, now settled at the bottom of the bucket. He was oblivious to the panic which was secretly welling up inside his dad. It was not easy to make much progress with the single stumpy oar that Graham was using. He tried alternate sides of the boat but the current was making better progress than he was and they seemed to be continuing further around the headland. He didn't have his mobile with him. He made it a strict policy, when on holiday, to leave it behind in the motor home and only check for messages each evening.

Sue and the girls were surprised to find that Graham and Max were still out when they got back from their shopping. They had enjoyed their day but suffice to say that the quality of shops had not resulted in the usual branded bags with which they would normally return. It was still afternoon so Sue decided to take a stroll along the shore with her binoculars to see if she could spot them. She walked a fair way but there was no sign of the dinghy and no sound of Max. She returned to the reception just to check with Phyllis that they had not returned and headed off elsewhere. They couldn't have gone far though, as she had the car. Phyllis hadn't seen them since they set off mid-morning but Sue still felt relaxed. Whenever Graham organised a boys' adventure for Max she knew that they often went missing for hours. She asked Natalie and Charlotte to join her as she decided to look in the opposite direction. The girls reluctantly accepted and they all agreed that, rather than go down to the shore, they would stay up higher and walk through the fields so that they could see further.

"I don't know why Dad didn't take his phone" said Charlotte with a hint of irritation "He always checks that we have got ours when we go out."

"Yes but your generation are permanently attached to them" replied Sue "Your father and I come on holiday for a bit of peace".

"It's quite peaceful without Max anyway" said Natalie. "They'll be back when it's time for dinner."

Somehow the longer they walked without any sign of the boys, the more worried they became although none of them wanted to own up to their feelings of increasing concern. They decided that it would probably be best to return to the site. The chances were that the boys would be back by now, looking for them. As they entered the site they came across Reg outside the steading.

"Hi Reg. You haven't seen Graham have you?" Sue asked anxiously.

"No, not since this morning" he replied. Immediately Reg thought about his advice to Graham about the currents and realised that the girls needed some assistance. He followed them around the shoreline and borrowed Sue's binoculars to look out to sea.

"Perhaps they moved off around the headland" he suggested as he knew that it followed the prevailing current. He instinctively knew that he should not mention the strength of the current for fear that it might arouse greater concern. "Tell you what" said Reg, "I'll ring my friend Angus. He's probably out in his boat checking his creels. He's sure to have spotted them."

Reg returned to his van to get his phone. He knew that Angus always took his mobile to sea with him just in case. Sure enough Angus was already on board about to set off from his own jetty just along the coast. Now that Sue and the girls were out of earshot Reg expressed his concern for Graham and Max in their small dinghy. He told Angus that as it was now nearly five o'clock they had been gone for over six hours and he felt sure that they should have returned by now. Angus could sense the urgency and instinctively knew that the current would have taken them around the headland. Thank goodness that the sea was still calm and the temperature kindly mild. Angus was only 10 minutes away from passing Camus and estimated that it would take him a further 20 minutes to round the headland. He was pleased to be told by Reg that Graham and Max had both been wearing bright yellow life jackets which would make them easier to spot, even from a distance.

By this time Graham had managed to reach a buoy far round the headland. He had tied the dinghy's rope to the buoy which had at least prevented them from drifting on further. His attempts to row back to Camus with a single pathetic oar were proving fruitless and were beginning to unsettle Max who, by now, had stopped watching Nemo and started to cry for Sue. By tying up the dinghy Graham was able to cuddle him and take some time to consider what to attempt next. After what seemed like ages, Graham could hear the distant sound of a boat engine which seemed to be coming from the Camus direction. He couldn't see anything though and the sound didn't seem to be getting any closer. He was tempted to call out but resisted for fear of alarming Max. Suddenly the sound, which had previously been subdued by the headland, changed and Angus's fishing boat came into view. Graham now called out.

"Hello there!" he called waving his arms about. "Wave to the fisherman" he said to Max.

As Reg had said, the sight of a man and boy in bright yellow life jackets gave Angus immediate confirmation that he had found them. He switched off his engine and drifted alongside. First he lifted Max on to his boat.

"Well my lad" he said with a smile, "what are you doing out here?"

"I'm fishing" replied Max innocently as he jumped down enthusiastically onto the solid floor of what seemed to him like an enormous ship.

"Am I glad to see you" said Graham whose appreciation and relief were obvious to see in his expression. Angus held out his strong hand to help him on board.

"Tie the dinghy up to the side of the boat and I'll take you back. Good job you found one of my buoys he said".

"Yes" replied Graham "God knows where we would have ended up if you hadn't come by. Oh by the way my name's Graham and this here is Max" only this time he gave Angus's hand a hearty shake.

"And I'm Angus. I got a call from Reg to report you both missing. I come out every evening to check my creels though I don't usually end up rescuing folk!"

Max was poking about in the old creel which Angus had inside the boat.

"Did you catch any fish?" Angus asked innocently.

"We caught Nemo. He's in my bucket" The bucket was of course still inside the dinghy. Somehow it didn't seem a priority when they had climbed on to Angus's boat.

"I don't catch fish" replied Angus "I catch lobsters."

Max wasn't sure what a lobster was but already he was looking expectantly at the wheel.

"While I'm here I might as well check out this creel" he said pulling up the line attached to the buoy and lifting it on to the deck. Max peered inside and saw a creature with enormous claws looking straight at him. He stepped back.

"My, that's a fine lobster you've caught for me" Angus chuckled. "Don't put your fingers in though 'cos he might snap them off."

Max studied the creature from a distance. Inside the creel were the monster lobster and two smaller crabs. He was fascinated. Angus quickly secured the lobster's front claws with strong rubber bands removing the danger to Max's fingers.

"Do you want to steer us home?" asked Angus.

Max climbed up onto the seat and took the wheel in both hands. He could only just see through the front window but fidgeted excitedly in the chair when the engine started and the boat went forward, the bow lifting up out of the water. Angus stood directly behind him making the necessary adjustments to the steering. Max was in his own little world. His imagination was racing, full of thoughts of this huge boat and how much he had to tell everyone when he got back. For the moment he was the captain and was racing to get away from the pirates who were chasing him in their smaller boat. The smaller boat was, of course, his dad's dinghy which had been tied to Angus's boat to be towed home. Suddenly Max remembered that Nemo was still in the dinghy. He must get home quickly to save him from the pirates!

On the return journey Angus phoned Reg to tell him that his mission had been successful and that the two lost souls were on their way back. He then took time to tell Graham about the tides and the currents and how many times he had himself got in to difficulty in these waters. He was making sure that Graham received the message that the sea on the west coast was not for the faint-hearted. Graham knew that he was indeed being given a subtle lecture but took no offence. Their rescue had already taught him that he had been both naïve and irresponsible and he felt suitably humble. Max's love of his boat and the sea had however encouraged Angus to offer to take them both out again on a proper fishing trip. His own son Donnie was 14 and was already on his Easter holidays from school: perhaps they would all have a boys' day out together.

They couldn't easily return to the slipway as Angus's boat could not reach the shallow approach. Instead they went back to his own jetty where Reg had agreed to meet them. As soon as they got off the boat, Angus headed straight back out to tend his creels. Max waved goodbye frantically. He couldn't wait to tell his mum all about his adventure. It was the best that he had ever had!

A fine specimen

Dishevelled heron

Leaving the harbour at Ulva

Oyster catcher

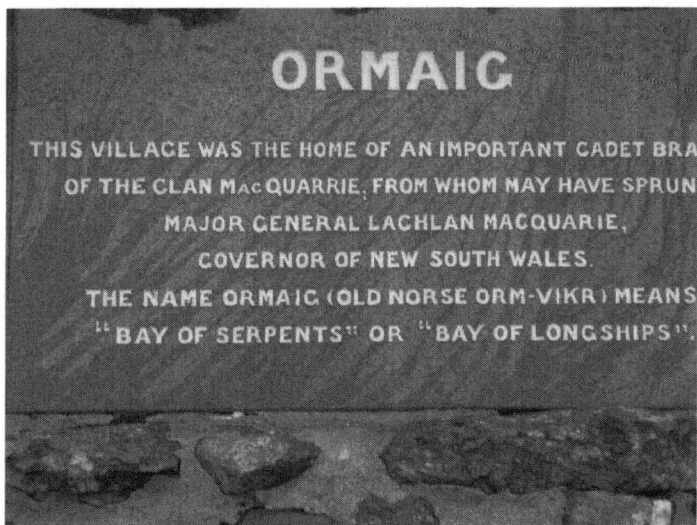

Plaque at Ormaig Ulva

Puffins on Lunga

Ruined croft Ormaig Ulva

The inspiation for 'Norman'

Thomas Telford Chuch Ulva

Tobermory

HIGHLAND CLEARANCES

OF COURSE IT was the same day that Chris and Melanie had been on their boat trip to see the puffins. They had therefore been out since early morning catching Jimmy's ferry to Mull. The ferry landed at Tobermory, which was in itself a picturesque sight with all its brightly coloured houses around the harbour. Strangely it looked a little like toy town, not surprising at it was the setting for the children's TV programme Balamory. Melanie loved it but didn't have much time to look around as the minibus taking them across the island to their next boat was already waiting. The young girl driving the bus had introduced herself as Gail. She was originally from south east England.

"What made you move here?" Melanie asked. She was intrigued.

"I studied marine biology at university in England" she replied over her shoulder, "then I was offered work experience with wildlife research on Mull. The people here are so friendly, the island is beautiful and the wildlife is simply amazing so I've never gone back home."

"What's it like in the winter though?" asked Chris.

"Well it's colder and wetter and there's not much work once the tourists have gone but I've got lots of friends here now and we still get some cracking days, even mid-winter."

She certainly knew how to drive the bus around the single track roads, anticipating every twist and turn and courteously pulling into a passing place on the very odd occasion that another vehicle was coming. There was clearly no risk here of getting stuck in traffic and missing the next boat.

"Have you been to the Treshnish Islands before?" she asked them.

"No but I've always wanted to see the puffins. Are they sure to be there?" replied Melanie.

"They've been returning to the island to breed since late March and are all very busy building their nests and getting ready to lay their egg" informed Gail.

"You said egg" picked up Melanie. "Do they only lay one?"

"Yes they make their nest underground in a burrow or in cracks in the boulders. They both take turns in incubating until the egg hatches in May. Although I prefer the sea mammals puffins are my favourite sea bird. They're affectionately known as seabird clowns 'cos they look so funny don't you think?"

"How long does it take to get to the island?" asked Chris.

"About two hours each way on the boat and then you get a good two hours ashore. I'll be there to meet you when you get back."

They finally came to the small jetty on the other side of the island. It was sleepy and peaceful, idyllically set in a small harbour offering quiet shelter for an assortment of old boats, each moored up to a buoy. Melanie was a touch concerned that one of these tiny vessels might be the one intending to take them to see the puffins. She couldn't imagine that they were robust enough to survive outside the harbour in the open sea. She needn't have worried though as a larger boat was approaching the jetty which had an open deck and a covered lower deck. The boat had 'Sea Adventures' written along the sides which confirmed that it was mooring up to welcome them on board. The two young men who were on board introduced themselves as Matt, the skipper, and David, the apprentice. It soon became apparent that David was far more than an apprentice. He too had graduated in marine biology and gladly shared his wealth of experience with his guests.

Today Chris and Melanie were the only passengers which meant that they enjoyed the undivided attention of both David and Matt for the whole day. On the outward journey they were told to look out for the sea birds, partly because of the variety that these waters offered but also because they acted as an early warning system for spotting any sea mammals should they be really lucky. David passed binoculars to them both and gave a constant running commentary of anything he could spot.

Melanie had, at first, thought that the comfort and comparative warmth of the lower deck looked quite appealing but both she and Chris were captivated by David's observations. They had seen gannets diving for fish, cormorants and seagulls landing and taking off and, as they got nearer to the Treshnish Isle of Lunga, they were excited to see puffins returning to their burrows high on the cliff top.

The two hours simply sped by. On the island was a small, floating jetty which had to be towed to the shore to enable the visitors to disembark. They then needed to climb over some rocks and then further up on to the grass above. David had already advised them to stay quiet and calm and to just find a spot near the puffins, sit down and have the camera ready. They hadn't needed to go far but did exactly as he had said.

They couldn't believe how tame the puffins were. Chris and Melanie simply sat by the burrows and watched the industrious activity going on all around them. Some were busy collecting nesting material maybe dried grass, tufts of heather or a prize twig. The puffins proudly carried their treasure back to the burrow. They all deployed a different stance, constantly on the look out, some stretching taller to look skyward probably watching out for gulls. Others scanned the territory, making sure that neighbours were oblivious to the progress they were making. The birds were certainly comic with their colourful beaks, a mix of orange red and yellow. They had bold, black eyes, a white face and portly white bellies contrasted with black wings. The overall appearance certainly revealed why they had the nickname of 'seabird clowns'. On land they often appeared clumsy sometimes waddling as if drunk, occasionally hopping or almost skipping which gave them added appeal. Melanie was observing every move they made but after looking at several face to face she couldn't help wondering who was studying whom! The puffins moved on from one spot to another occasionally heading back out to sea presumably to feed. Melanie had been hoping to see them return with beaks full of sand eels but, as they had no young to feed, they simply returned, wings flapping, to resume their activity. Their landings were extremely unpredictable some graceful whilst others revealed a real sense of panic. Perhaps those anticipating a crash landing were less experienced. Frequently they could be seen squabbling with neighbours and going about their determined business. Good job Chris had a digital camera as they were compelled to take endless photos to record this wonderful day. Melanie simply sat and took it all in. She felt so calm and relaxed and felt that she could stay on Lunga for hours. She particularly enjoyed the strange sounds coming from down, deep in the burrows. It was a curious sound, somewhat quizzical; a strange deep throated call as if they had found something below which puzzled them.

When it came time to depart the pair were equally keen to see what might await them on the return journey. Sadly there were no sightings of dolphins or whales on this occasion but they were not disappointed. How could they be? They had shared a special wedding present and seen wildlife so intimately that the memory would be sure to stay with them forever.

Gail and the minibus were waiting for them as they drifted back in to the harbour. Melanie told her everything they had seen, not realising that she had heard similar stories many times over. Gail said that had their visit been later, say June or July, they would almost certainly have seen the chicks before they are abandoned by their parents in early August. Melanie loved the name 'puffling' which Gail informed her was the name given to the cute, fluffy, grey babies who do not have the colourful features of the adults until later on.

"Well maybe next time" said Melanie hopefully "We'll make the trip a bit later on."

On the way back on Jimmy's ferry, they looked at the pictures they had taken and spotted those special shots which would be sure to make it to their honeymoon album.

When they finally got back to Camus, Reg and Phyllis had closed the reception after the eventful day on site. Chris and Melanie looked forward to entering the recommendation of their excursion in the visitor book which Phyllis had made available in reception the next day. They would certainly give it five stars!

The next day Mick and Maureen were all packed up and ready to leave. They came to say farewell and to give Phyllis the finished painting of the reception festooned with her colourful hanging baskets. Overwhelmed by the gift, she politely insisted that Maureen should keep it, even though she had already envisaged that it would hang on the wall directly behind the counter, where all future guests would be sure to see it. The two ladies had, in spite of the short stay, made good friends; something that both Reg and Phyllis would come to learn was a natural benefit of their job as wardens. Before they left, Mick was pleased to make another booking for early September, making them the first official return booking. Reg hoped that this would indeed be the first of many.

So much drama, and yet this was still only the start of their first season. From that day on visitor numbers increased. Easter was usually the real start but as each month went by more visitors arrived. The website designed by Elaine was now active and the leaflets which Phyllis had taken to the tourist offices and surrounding businesses were also attracting customers.

Time had passed so quickly and as Reg looked out across the now familiar but constantly beautiful sea, he was reminiscing about the two previous seasons and the many unusual guests and noteworthy stories he had to tell. He never tired of his life as a warden and looked forward to every approaching season as if it were his first. Every year he had a list of jobs prepared. The winter always took its toll on the site and its facilities and as he; breathed in the clean, crisp air he started his obligatory inspection, clipboard and pencil to the ready.

As he conducted his usual tour he was mindful to look out for any scrapes in the ground revealing the spent nests of oyster catchers so numerous along this shore. Over the last few seasons Reg had learnt a lot about the wildlife of Camus. For example he now knew that the same pairs were likely to return again this season as there is particularly strong mate and site fidelity in these birds, with many pairs defending the same site for a number of years. A single nesting is normal, timed over the summer months. Reg had gained this knowledge partly from the books he had read but mostly from the regular visits made to the site by bird enthusiasts from around the world.

He had particularly enjoyed, Geoffrey and Ronnie, the two gentlemen who came each summer, lured by the sight of golden eagles soaring above the craggy outcrops inland and, in particular, by the rarer sea eagle famously researched on the Isle of Mull. They were older gentlemen in their 70s but both were still very fit and spritely. They came for a week each year, sharing a smart caravan and taking turns to drive, cook and do all the usual chores. Reg smiled to himself at the looks they frequently got from other guests. After all, it was unusual for two men to holiday together, particularly sharing a caravan. In reality they were both widowers who had been friends since they left school. Their mutual circumstance had led to them spending time, and now holidaying, together.

They regularly took Jimmy's ferry to Mull and spent hours watching and taking amazing photos of the sea eagles soaring over Loch Na Keal. Having been re-introduced to the neighbouring Isle of Rum in the late 70s the birds had made Mull their fortress and were now a huge draw for ornithologists visiting the island. No wonder as they are, after all, the largest bird of prey to be found on the British Isles. From head to talon they stand at a metre high sporting dark brown plumage with the famous white tail feathers, hence their name. Geoffrey had some wonderful video footage of the female sweeping down over the loch surface and grasping a huge fish in her powerful talons which she proudly carried back to the nest. The sea eagles were majestic and sat in the tall pine trees with regal poise as if they were looking down on their kingdom. They have no natural predators other than man who might steal their valuable eggs but fortunately Mull has wildlife experts who keep a regular check on both the birds and their nest sites. Geoffrey's footage showed clearly that they do, regularly, endure harassment from mobbing crows, clearly none too happy with their presence. Whist soaring effortlessly on their two and a half metre wingspan they often disappear in to the clouds soaring ever upwards above the mountain ridges of Ben More. The crows seem to deploy a tactic of diving at the eagle attempting to scare it away. As if it would indeed be scared but such a minor irritation! Nevertheless the tactic sometimes works as the eagle gracefully moves on to more peaceful skies.

Reg found it particularly amusing when other visitors too quickly decided that Geoffrey and Ronnie, holidaying as a pair, seemed rather strange. One such memorable visitor was a single chap who arrived on site in a tired and rusty jeep. He looked well travelled with grey hair tied back in a crude pony tail. He came to reception and asked if he could park his 'camper' for a few nights. His was dressed in camouflage clothing and reminded Phyllis of the famous TV presenter who hunted, cooked and slept in wilder areas. He initially parked next to Geoffrey and Ronnie. In his Jeep he had a small camping stove and a rollout mattress and sleeping bag, simple but functional. Each morning he would put on his oversized backpack and disappear for most of the day, sometimes in to the evening. He came to the site shop every day for bread and milk but nothing else. Phyllis thought that he had maybe brought a store of provisions with him in his Jeep but whenever he returned he seemed to have caught his dinner for the day - maybe a rabbit, a pheasant, some crabs or fish. He liked to cook his food outside but didn't have a BBQ with charcoal and firelighters so he set up a small circle of stones upon which he laid wood he had brought back from his foraging.

Reg watched him light it up the first time. He had expected to see him rub sticks together in true 'survival' style and was somewhat disappointed when he pulled a box of matches from his pocket. Reg's sign which advised guests that BBQs were permitted did not indeed specify that what was expected was a self-contained modern BBQ on legs. He was worried about the charring on the ground that would await the next arrivals to the pitch.

'Survival Man', as Reg had secretly called him, liked to display his manly attributes. Every morning, come rain or shine, he would take a dip in the sea, swimming a fair way out before returning to his 'van' to dry off. He didn't seem to use the men's shower block at all for some reason, other than to respect the call of nature. Once dry, he would do a series of press ups outside his van. These exercises were done to impress in the hope that the size of his muscles were available for everyone to admire. Reg smiled to himself. His army friends had a strength and courage which went well beyond 'Survival Man's' token gestures. In the improvised shower blocks hastily erected at each army camp he had witnessed muscles toned by sustained physical exertion which surpassed those displayed by 'Survival Man' many times over.

Every morning the two older gentlemen would step out of their van and head to the shower block, toiletry bag and towel ready. They returned to share breakfast, outside if the weather was fine and always said good morning to their neighbour. He acknowledged them but that was all. He carefully avoided further conversation. One morning they couldn't resist approaching him to find out more about the food he had been seen eating.

"How do you do?" Geoffrey said "I hope that this doesn't sound rude but we've been watching you for the last few days and couldn't resist asking you about the 'game' you bring back each evening".

'Survival Man' felt very uncomfortable with this outnumbered approach.

"We were out bird watching and caught sight of you in our scope" said Ronnie.

'Survival Man' was immediately alarmed at the thought that, unbeknown to him, he had been secretly observed as he went about his business.

"We saw you snare a rabbit yesterday in the field across the way" Ronnie admitted indicating the direction along the coast.

With a tinge of guilt, 'Survival Man' knew that the rabbit had been caught a fair distance away and quickly realised that his every move had clearly been watched by these imposing neighbours.

"Well yes, I catch all my own meat and forage for wild mushrooms and other vegetation in fact I'm off in a minute to see what's about today. I'm heading off across the hills and into the forest for a change!" He thought that he would venture further hoping that this might extend beyond the range of their spotting scope.

"We see you take an early swim each morning. I bet the water's cold" said Geoffrey wanting to prolong the conversation.

"No, not at all" replied 'Survival Man' in a deep, husky voice "I've swum a lot further in colder waters than these many times" he boasted as if to add to his rough, tough aura.

"Do you need a licence for hunting game around here?" asked Geoffrey innocently.

"No, it's only small animals I take" he replied tentatively but not really sure whether they had a point. "Anyway must away now. Hope you have a nice day". He stepped back inside his Jeep, picked up his backpack complete with compass, OS map, binoculars and sack for his intended kill and hurriedly headed off the site with great speed.

Geoffrey and Ronnie would have stayed and chatted longer had the opportunity been afforded. They had thought that a man holidaying alone might welcome some company but 'Survival Man' seemed nervous and anxious to avoid prolonged dialogue. Perhaps he simply lacked the art of social conversation.

Today they were planning a trip to Ulva which was known to afford the opportunity for some rarer bird sightings. They were hoping to see the widgeon, maybe the pied flycatcher and a supposed sighting of a corncrake thought to now be on the island. They carried with them binoculars, a spotting scope and some serious camera equipment. Reg had been given the opportunity to look at their photos which looked so professional. Ronnie had kindly sent him some prints following their last visit which were on display in their visitor book. They were both true gentlemen who lived near Norfolk but loved their holidays on Scotland's west coast. It was true that the Norfolk countryside and coast offered them regular opportunities to pursue their shared hobby but Camus always enticed them back for sightings not available back home. This particular morning they had yet another surprise for Phyllis as they came into the reception. It was the most amazing photo of the barn owl as it left the steading to venture out across the fields. They must have been facing the wonderfully distinctive heart shaped face as they had caught it full on, wings curving gracefully down and the full array of its plumage with pure white under parts and speckled wing tips leading to soft brown feathers on the upper wing. The picture was as good as any they had seen in RSPB calendars, magazines etc. They described how it had flown so silently from the site. Apparently tiny serrations on the edges of its flight feathers break up the flow of air over its wings, thereby reducing the noise that accompanies other birds. Reg was always impressed by the detailed knowledge that they had. When they showed the photo to him his mind was working overtime. Would future visitors appreciate the opportunity to see these wonderful birds, so close around the site?

As soon as Geoffrey and Ronnie left the site, heading for Jimmy's ferry, Reg noticed 'Survival Man' emerge from the trees surrounding the site and thought perhaps he had forgotten something - but not at all. His impromptu return was solely for the purpose of re-siting his Jeep. At the time Reg was puzzled as to why he had decided to move. The pitch he had chosen had a great view and he had seemed settled there for several days' now: indeed he was due to leave in a couple of day's time. He chose a different pitch on the far side of Camus. As Reg busied himself, emptying the bins, he walked past 'Survival Man' and couldn't resist checking that everything was in order.

"I see you've decided to move" he stated "Is everything ok for you?"

"Yes, fine" replied 'Survival Man', a touch uncomfortably. "I prefer this pitch. Those chaps next to me are a bit odd don't you think?"

Reg smiled, partly because in his opinion it was 'Survival Man' himself whose attire and whose activities came across as unusual.

"They are fine gentlemen" he replied "they've been here several times before."

Having been in the army, he was conscious that any suspicion of improper conduct would be quickly spotted and assumed that 'Survival Man' had jumped to a hasty but wholly incorrect conclusion.

"It's very sad that they have both lost their wives but they seem to get such pleasure from walking and spotting the rare birds. They are both knowledgeable ornithologists and a real pleasure to engage in conversation. They've even given us copies of some photos which we've put on display"

"I suppose that's why they carry a spotting scope" 'Survival Man' replied realising that he had perhaps misjudged them and wondering what reason he might offer them later for his change of pitch.

"I was a bit worried that my BBQs were perhaps interfering with other caravanners so I moved over here away from everybody else" he thought quickly.

Reg let it appear that he had accepted this explanation but had a further concern that 'Survival Man's' actions in hunting local game might be illegal and that, if this was the case, it might reflect badly for the site in the future. Being a responsible warden, he thought that he should check this out.

Later that day, Reg saw Angus approaching with a distinctly solemn looking 'Survival Man' by his side.

"Afternoon Reg" Angus greeted.

"Hello there Angus, Another lovely day. Do you want to carry on with Fergal today?" Reg asked.

Fergal was the Gaelic name given to the Fordson by Angus's father. It means 'man of strength'.

"Ok in a wee while" said Angus firmly directing the camouflaged man back to his Jeep. "I'll make my way to the steading then," giving a clear indication to Reg that he wanted to talk privately.

Once inside the steading Angus's voice took an angry tone.

"Who is that idiot? Did you know he's been poaching on my land and on the estate? Good job that I caught him. Niall would have almost certainly prosecuted. I've already told him that I'm thinking about taking it further."

Reg had never seen Angus so angry.

"Who's Niall" he asked.

"The estate head stalker and a very good friend of mine" explained Angus.

Reg invited Angus back to his van to make him a soothing cuppa.

"I found him setting up snares over in my fields" he said raising his voice yet again. "Mind you he won't be doing it anymore that's for sure. Sorry Reg but I've told him he'd better leave before I prosecute. Oh and by the way, I've confiscated the hare he just caught!"

Eventually Angus calmed down and resumed his more expected friendly manner.

"I wondered whether he was allowed to catch game" Reg said "but assumed that he had checked it was ok. I'm really sorry Angus. I'll be sure to put a notice in the office although most people come here to admire the wildlife, not kill it."

Angus told him that in Scotland it is an offence to go onto someone's land without seeking their permission to hunt any type of game.

"I could have had him arrested him you know."

After tea they spent a good couple of hours working on Fergal, laughing at Angus's encounter with 'Survival Man'. How Reg would have loved to have been there: after all, he was not averse to a little confrontation himself. Reg told him about 'Survival Man's' weird habits and confessed that he would not be unhappy to see the back of him. By the time they came back out, the reprimanded visitor had already left.

"He certainly didn't take long in packing up" said Reg "You must have put the wind up him!"

"Och good riddance to bad rubbish" scoffed Angus "He'll no mess with an angry Scotsman again!"

When Reg returned to his van he met a baffled Phyllis, intent on telling him that one of their guests had left early.

"I know" announced Reg "Angus caught him poaching on his land and sent him packing. I think that if I'd seen Angus that angry, I'd have been on my way too" he laughed.

"But he'd already paid for two more nights" said Phyllis

"He would have paid more than that if Angus had prosecuted him" replied Reg. "Apparently it's illegal to hunt game on other people's land. I was wondering when I saw what he was up to. I didn't like to see it but now I know I'll put some signs up".

"Don't you think that's a bit reactionary dear?" suggested Phyllis "No other visitors have even contemplated poaching."

When Geoffrey and Ronnie returned from their trip to the island they noticed that their neighbour had moved on.

"He didn't say he was leaving today but then he didn't say much at all" remarked Ronnie.

"A slight disagreement with our neighbour" Phyllis let slip "Apparently he was poaching game from his land and was asked, or should I say told, to leave. I don't know if you've seen Angus but he's a bit like the incredible hulk - you know that saying 'You wouldn't like me when I'm angry!'

Before the season ended Reg took himself off to his workshop to make an assortment of bird houses. Inspired by Geoffrey and Ronnie he was now very much aware that guests coming to Camus were invariably very fond of the wildlife that was all around. If he were able to attract more birds that would be sure to please their future guests. Geoffrey had told him that the type of birds, which might use a bird box included the robin, wren, pied wagtail, spotted flycatcher and black redstart. He had also made up a large bird table which he would place just outside the reception. The boxes were all completed and positioned before they returned home. If any nesting birds were to be tempted the boxes would need to be put in place before they left.

SOME GUESTS ARE WELCOME.
SOME NOT!

AS REG STROLLED down to the old boathouse, now a little more weather-beaten than it was when he first arrived at Camus, his head was already full of the plans he had drafted, together with Angus, to start up a sea kayaking operation. Donnie was now seventeen and was soon to leave school. He had a real passion for the activity and, although it was fairly seasonal he was mindful to start both taster sessions and day trips for tourists. There was little employment opportunity for local youngsters and Angus's croft and lobster fishing was no big earner. Although the Camus bookings had increased incrementally over the years, Reg, Phyllis and Elaine had considered that introducing a new facility to the site would attract more, younger visitors.

Reg had prepared the expected task list which started with the removal of the old twisted roof and the replacement of much of the rotten wood. Inside, the boathouse was the size of a large garage. When the tide came in it only entered the structure for the first few meters and half the boathouse remained dry enough to erect a structure for storing a number of kayaks. Angus had sent him some dimensions over the Christmas holiday and Reg had designed a tiered system for which he would use scaffold poles and wooden slats.

Last Christmas had seen Meg coming to stay with them in Worcester. She had travelled down from Oban by overnight train and stayed for several days. Phyllis was so looking forward to her visit and the opportunity to show her where they lived for what was now a short four months of the year. It soon seemed, however, that whenever they were together, the conversation always reverted to Camus and what was now a shared passion for the west coast. They visited Cheltenham and Oxford and introduced Meg to their friends and family. Phyllis loved the opportunity to return the compliment of home-cooked food although she felt a little daunted by Meg's ability to make the most sumptuous dish from fairly basic ingredients. For Christmas dinner, Phyllis had bought all the vegetables from the local farm shop and ordered a turkey from the butcher in her village. There were eight for dinner on Christmas day Meg, Reg, Phyllis, their daughter Annie, her husband Craig and their five year old granddaughter Ellie; also joining them was their son Ryan who had just returned from his tour of duty in the middle-east and finally Phyllis's elderly father Henry, who was now 94 years old and very frail. Phyllis had always enjoyed Christmas particularly, since their granddaughter had arrived. The pile of presents under the tree was so typical of the modern trend to indulge and yet, since spending time at Camus, they had become accustomed to simpler pleasures which required no credit cards or fancy wrapping.

The dinner was thoroughly enjoyed by everyone and Meg laughed hysterically at the Wii games she was encouraged to attempt. Before the family left Ellie sat on Meg's lap and begged for another story of Norman and his adventures. Meg was a natural at story telling. She based her stories partly on Norman's antics and partly on a healthy embellishment of description which clearly appealed to Ellie. Henry had fallen asleep in the chair by early evening so Reg had taken him back to his own bungalow just a short distance away. It was quite late when the others went, leaving Phyllis, Reg and Meg to tidy up and sit down to enjoy the peace and tranquillity that all three were more used to.

Meg was returning home the day after Boxing Day and confessed that, whilst she had enjoyed her stay immensely, she couldn't wait to get back home. The traffic and hustle of life here down south and the trappings of modern living would never entice her to leave her home. This was the first 'holiday' she had had for over 20 years and yet, strangely, she felt a longing to return home to relax. The three of them discussed her feelings although both Reg and Phyllis could already identify the same sentiments for themselves. Phyllis was aware that their Worcestershire bungalow now, sadly, took second place. Reg was mindful that his garden was no longer what it used to be. They had a regular gardener who came to keep the grass cut, the weeds checked and the shrubs trimmed back. It looked neat and tidy but lacked the love and attention they both used to invest.

"Do you think you'll ever sell this house?" asked Meg politely.

"The trouble is that we're not getting any younger" replied Reg "I'm going to be 65 this year and there will come a day when we can't be wardens anymore, then we'll need a home to return to."

"Reg has done so much here" carried on Phyllis "If we do stop being wardens I can't see the point of him starting all over again."

And so the bungalow was cleaned up, packed away and left once again for the new season at Camus. They no longer towed their own van between Camus and Worcester. Instead Reg had increased the height of his large workshop door and carefully stored it away for the winter months.

Following his task list, Reg started to remove the boathouse roof and construct his kayak storage inside. From the assortment of fish bones, mussel and crab shells that were littered across the floor, it was clear that the otter had made regular use of the structure. They had only seen it themselves on a handful of occasions but several visitors had managed to take photos. The best photo had been taken by Geoffrey, whilst sitting quietly along the shore observing an envious heron. It was the classic image of the otter floating on his back devouring a velvet crab. The beautiful photograph was clear evidence of the quality of the camera he used, revealing each distinct whisker and the characteristic pale underbelly. Obviously he had used a high quality zoom which gave the impression that the otter was close. In reality it was probably some distance away as it always avoided people at all costs. All the same, it gave visitors the hope that they too might see it if they looked carefully. Reg hadn't seen where its holt was but had every reason to think that it was close by. Otters need a supply of fresh water to keep their coats clean and the small burn which ran under the humped-back bridge to the sea was an obvious source.

At the start of the summer, two beautifully restored VW camper vans arrived, bringing six young students, all boys, from Edinburgh University. Reg welcomed them with particular interest. He and Phyllis had such a van many, many years ago. It was an old split-screen camper, very much sought after now. He loved to see that the younger generation still appreciated this iconic vehicle and the freedom and fun that came with it. They parked next to each other and cleverly fixed an awning in the gap between them, under which they were able to pass the evenings with more than a few beers. The students were the active type who set off each morning with proper hiking boots and backpacks. They told Reg that they often walked at least 15 miles each day and had managed the Galmadale round in seven hours, which was hard going. They had arrived just as Reg, Angus and Donnie had bought four kayaks to start the new venture. What great timing it turned out to be: the lads couldn't resist the opportunity to give kayaking a try and Donnie was pleased that his first customers were all fit and confident lads up for a laugh.

Of course, he had completed the necessary courses to qualify him as a trainer but as he was just starting, he lacked the experience of supervising others. Whilst they were older than he they respectfully listened to the instructions he gave. He took them out in two groups staying close to the shore line and paddling around the bay, adding extra fun on the return journey by suggesting a race back to the boathouse. This engendered the competitive spirit in the lads and added to the excitement. They clearly enjoyed the experience and booked a further session with Donnie before their week was out.

To add to the attraction, some of Donnie's friends came to see the start of his business. They were lads and lassies from all around. They brought tents with them, clearly intending to pitch up. Reg and Phyllis had not expected many campers but welcomed the enthusiasm they brought to the site. Being that they were local youngsters, Phyllis suggested that they should not charge the full fee but simply a contribution for their use of the showers.

The presence of six unattached young lads was obviously a real draw and Camus was soon alive each evening with music, laughter and wild parties. The kayaks were out every day although Reg doubted that Donnie was making much money. It turned out that he had negotiated a deal with them which involved the students placing pictures and messages about the kayaking on Facebook in the hope that word would spread and others might be encouraged to come and try the experience for themselves. Perhaps Donnie had the makings of a proper business man or maybe it was the result of his mum's marketing experience. Either way it didn't matter because from that first week on, the sea kayaking became a real attraction for the site.

One of the less loved recurring visitors to Camus were the dreaded midges. They arrived in May and lasted through the summer to September. They may be tiny by comparison to their cousins inhabiting further south but their thirst for blood and their persistence in extracting it resulted in many unwary caravan visits to Camus being the first and only. Phyllis had stocked the shop well with the recommended bog myrtle essential oil, the Avon products, plug-in midge repellents, after-bite soothers and, of course, a supply of midge nets which proved particularly popular. It was perhaps the most topical conversation shared by many a guest to the reception throughout the summer. When the site was full, it was amusing to watch the frenzied actions of both adults and children, all trying to keep the beasties away. Of course they seemed to wait particularly for the early evening when most people were trying to sit outside enjoying their BBQ and the splendid views. In reality, they were around most of the time but appeared to be determined to maximise their nuisance potential when people were trying to relax at the end of the day. Citronella candles were one of the best sellers in Phyllis's shop and more orders for midge nets had been placed every season.

Mention of the midges always reminded Phyllis of the memorable invasion of 'the pikies'! It was mid summer that the couple arrived. They pulled up with a caravan which was seemingly held together by endless amounts of brown parcel tape. The outside was covered in green streaks, indicating that it was kept somewhere hidden deep in vegetation. The nicotine stained curtains inside were further evidence that the couple's disregard for cleanliness applied to all areas. A woman, whose age was difficult to judge from her overweight and unkempt appearance, came into reception and asked for a pitch for a week. She signed in as Mrs Jackson and unfortunately filled the office with the unpleasant, stale aroma that you might normally associate with someone who is clearly in need of a good bath. As they pulled away in search of a pitch, Reg hurried to direct them to the far side of the field. There were not many pitches left but fortunately a pitch to the rear of the site, partly masked by some gorse bushes was available.

"I'm afraid that all the other pitches have been pre-booked. My wife should have told you" he continued intending to have words with Phyllis as soon as he had executed his damage limitation strategy.

As Mr Jackson jerkily reversed the van into its spot, his Bedford van let out plumes of smoke, temporarily filling the immediate area with a haze uncharacteristic for Camus. Reg did not stop to pass the usual pleasantries, which greeted most new arrivals, instead he made haste to the reception to discuss the matter with Phyllis.

"Why did you let them in?" he snapped angrily.

"How could I refuse" responded Phyllis anticipating an argument.

"You should have said that we were full. God knows what our other guests will think. I've managed to direct them to the pitch on the far side so at least they are out of view from any new arrivals."

"Why don't you just go and tell them that their van isn't up to Camus standards?" added Phyllis sarcastically.

"Of course I can't say that" replied Reg.

"Well now you understand the position I was in when they booked in. They've paid just like everyone else" she added.

"They look like a real pair of pikies" grumbled Reg.

"Actually, gypsies look after their vans" Phyllis corrected him "From the look of the woman, she seemed to be in a worse state than the caravan."

"Their old van is billowing out exhaust as well. I've never seen anything like it. How long have they booked for?" he asked hoping desperately that it was only a short stay.

"They've paid for a week" answered Phyllis expecting a further explosion from Reg.

"Strooth!" exclaimed Reg. This was his usual phrase when he was exasperated by something. "I just hope that we don't lose business as a result of this" he muttered as he left the office, leaving Phyllis with the distinct feeling that this was, in his mind, all her fault.

As Reg went past the Jackson's on his way to shut himself off in the steading and calm down he could hear them arguing already. They were levelling and unloading the van. There was no smart aqua roll to use for water: instead they had an old army water container all bashed and dented. Their chairs were the simple fold-up picnic type, saggy with the weight imposed by Mrs Jackson but, completely out of character, they unpacked a brand new porch awning which Mr Jackson was beginning to erect. Fortunately this made an immediate improvement to their pitch although it took some time for Mr Jackson to work it all out. Mrs Jackson was very vocal and coarse and less than kind to her husband, irritated by the delay in erecting the awning and the resulting obstruction to the doorway;

"Just hurry up. You're nothing but a boy scout" she shouted from inside the van. Reg cringed but decided to keep well away.

The pair kept themselves to themselves as the week went slowly past. Reg had vainly hoped that Mr Jackson might wash the caravan. Perhaps he had brought it away direct from storage but, as he suspected there was no attempt made to improve the appearance. The midges were in full force now and had, unlike Reg taken a real liking to Mrs Jackson. Perhaps the unkempt hair offered them a safe refuge but, unfortunate though it was for her, she certainly experienced their full wrath one evening. She was asleep in her chair outside the van as dusk was falling when she felt a tingling across her face which woke her up. At first she simply brushed her hand across her cheek but soon the brushing became more frantic across the whole of her face and neck. She struggled to prise herself out of the chair.

"Can't you give me a hand rather than watch like a useless idiot" she snapped at Mr Jackson.

"Help with what?" he answered.

"Something is crawling all over me" she exclaimed "what is it?" She made her way inside her caravan but unfortunately that was no escape. A veritable swarm of midges had landed in her untidy hair while she was asleep, so many that it felt as if she had walked in to a spiders web. By retreating to her van she had simply infected the caravan even more than it was before. She finally rushed to the shower block from which she eventually emerged a changed woman. For the first time that week she looked clean and tidy albeit just as grumpy as before. The very next day she came to the shop and bought a midge net. Success all round and a positive vote for the midges.

When Meg heard the story she laughed "You know that it is the female midges that attack" she informed them.

"Well the boys had more sense to stay away" Reg laughed from behind his Highland News.

"You ken that they can inflict more than 3,000 bites in an hour. How long do you think that she had been asleep for?" Meg asked.

"I've no idea" replied Phyllis but the midges clearly managed to entice her to the shower which was more than Mr Jackson had managed for a long time."

"Well I was hoping that they had no intentions of returning" added Reg "Now I'm convinced that they won't come back."

They often exchanged stories about the oddities of their guests. Meg's B&B business had steady visitors through the summer months. She particularly remembered the timid, middle-aged couple for whom she had to organise a local search party when they went missing one day. They had decided to go for a walk which they had picked out from a book of walks in the area. Had Meg realised that they had not got the full OS map and a compass, she would have advised them that these tourist walking books were, in themselves, insufficient. The couple had set off after a hearty breakfast of bacon, eggs, mushrooms, haggis and black pudding. The sky was clear and the sun was shining but she had told them that the weather was due to change later that afternoon, so they packed a jacket, believing that to be a sensible move.

It was mid-afternoon when the wind picked up and the rain started. It persisted for a good couple of hours. They had shown Meg the walk that they had planned to take.

According to the book it should have taken between four and five hours. They had started at 10am and Meg had hoped that, by the time the rain started, they might well have been on the return leg. However, as many walkers will know, estimates of time published alongside walking routes are nearly always underestimated. The publishers seem to always assume that everyone is young and super fit and doesn't stop on route to either admire the views or partake of a delicious sandwich made with Meg's own homemade bread. Therefore when evening came and the couple had not returned at the expected time for their evening meal, which Meg had previously agreed to prepare, she became rather concerned. She knew where they had planned to go and so, after leaving a note on the kitchen table, she got into her car hoping that they might at least be making their way along the road.

Of course it was possible that the couple were still off road but with her binoculars at hand and her knowledge of the local area, she thought that she might be able to spot them from one of the vantage points she stopped en route. The rain was still coming down though not as hard as it had been late afternoon. It was already well gone 6 o'clock and they had been gone now for more than eight hours. The roads in that area did not offer drivers a wide choice of directions so although Meg ventured where she could in her 4x4 Landrover, she failed to spot them. She returned to Taigh Meg and rang both Phyllis and Angus to see whether either had, by chance, spotted them. No-one had seen them but Angus rang Niall to see whether he had seen them, as their walk intended to take them through a part of the estate. As the time was passing, Angus arranged for himself and Reg to borrow a couple of the quad bikes, used on the estate, and organise a search party. Niall offered to join them. It was so typical of the local people to respond to the possible plight of their visitors in such a way, much as Angus had done when finding little Max and Graham marooned on his buoy.

Reg started the quad bike with his usual confidence but the bumpy terrain combined with his advancement of years made the search somewhat uncomfortable. They were looking for almost an hour when they eventually came across the lost couple. Elated to have been found at last they looked a sad and sorry pair. As predicted, they had wandered a way off their intended trail and were now heading in the completely opposite direction to Meg's steading. Their inadequate coats were soaked through, as were their boots and trousers. Both were tired and had contemplated a night of 'wild camping' but without the necessary tent, provisions and dry clothes. They were so pleased to see the rescue party and gladly sat pillion allowing Reg and Angus to return them back home. Of course, they wanted to recompense them for all their time and trouble but neither Angus nor Reg would hear of it.

A few of Reg and Phyllis's friends had come to visit them, staying at Meg's as most did not have a caravan of their own. In this way, Meg's business had benefitted from the extra visits. This year Annie, Craig and Ellie had come for a week at the start of the summer holidays. Ellie was now nearly seven and had been at school for two years. What an amazing week they had. Ellie had been looking forward to this since Easter in expectation of yet more stories of Norman given to her each bedtime by an enthusiastic Meg.

Angus arranged to take them all on a boat trip, leaving Donnie in charge of the site. They couldn't have arranged it better if they'd tried. The sea was calm and Reg had told them all, especially Ellie, to look out for the birds, the seals and anything else they might spot. She sat on Phyllis's lap, looking over the side with her Barbie binoculars pressed firmly in her eye sockets. Annie and Craig too were transfixed by every bird and animal they picked up using bins borrowed from Reg and Phyllis. Occasionally one of them spotted an inquisitive seal popping its head above the water. They called to each, other pointing in the appropriate direction. Ellie loved to give them all names which came from her favourite TV show Dora the Explorer. She called the first she spotted Dora and two others Boots and Backpack. Angus stopped at one of his creels, lifting it to show his passengers what was inside. Fortunately he was in luck; a good sized lobster was trapped inside which Angus would collect later. He lifted it out, telling Ellie to watch out for the claws which were snapping in defence.

"I'm going to call him Swiper" she said, impressing them all with her choice of name and making her nanny and granddad proud.

A way off, Angus could see the tell-tale sign of gulls gathering which might indicate that dolphins were on the hunt. He turned his boat and made his way in that direction.

Sure enough, as they got closer they could see the dorsal fins moving swiftly, forming a seemingly crazed posse. Some were jumping briefly above the surface in excitement. They seemed to be hunting, circling the fish and then forcing them up to the surface. There must have been more than a dozen working as a team to maximise their catch. The binoculars were being passed around to give everyone the chance to watch. Ellie offered her pair to Meg who, of course, accepted graciously. Angus cut his engines and allowed the boat to drift in the immediate area. The spectacle lasted for at least 20 minutes. According to Angus they were bottlenose dolphins quite common in the waters in these parts. Everyone on the boat was delighted with the experience even Angus who had seen the dolphins many times.

As they made their way back to Angus's jetty, a much larger fin could be seen above the water, moving slowly but continuously along the shoreline. Angus once again cut his engines and steered the boat alongside. It was a relatively rare sighting of a basking shark but the calmness of the water allowed them to see clearly that it was almost the same length as Angus's boat, probably about eight meters long. It was a bluish, greyish colour with a long, almost pointed snout. Typically it was peacefully drifting with its huge mouth wide open catching the minute plankton found along these shores, courtesy of the Gulf Stream. The gaping mouth was big enough to swallow Ellie in one gulp or indeed, any of the adults but in spite of its size, it posed no risk to the captivated party. Ellie tried to lean over the side to touch it but she couldn't reach. Donnie had, by all accounts, managed last year to get a short tow whilst paddling in his kayak. Craig and Annie were amazed. They had already seen so much beauty and wildlife on this holiday. They were beginning to understand why Reg and Phyllis were enjoying life there so much. When they returned and it was time for bed, Ellie asked Meg whether she could have a different story to the usual adventures of Norman and so Meg hastily made up a story about a huge but friendly shark called Benny, who took Donnie and his kayak out for a picnic one day.

Before they left Camus, Donnie took Annie and Craig out in the kayaks for a couple of hours leaving nanny and granddad in charge. Ellie loved to explore the site and particularly enjoyed sitting on Fergal which was, by now, granddad's pride and joy. Of course it was sad when their week at Meg's was coming to an end: after this they were heading further north to Loch Ness. Ellie really wanted to see the monster but the adults were repeatedly telling her that the monster was very hard to see. Meg had a DVD called Loch Ness which was a family film often watched by visitors with children. It told of a little girl who could see and talk to the monster who hid from almost everyone else. Ellie was convinced that she was that little girl and Phyllis just hoped that she would not be too disappointed.

The rest of that summer was quiet. Annie and Craig had been so lucky to visit when they did because the end of July, August and September were wet and miserable. Most of the pre-booked guests arrived as planned but the referrals from the tourist office were considerably reduced and some were leaving earlier than planned in order to seek improved climes further south. Even Reg and Phyllis became a little depressed as each day broke with a return of grey, cloud ridden skies. Donnie's kayak trips were continuing well, presumably his clients expected to get wet. Meg had also seen a drop in visitors and it was uncharacteristically becoming a real topic of conversation.

In late September, Reg received a letter from Touring Haven holidays which landed like a bombshell in the site office. The letter forewarned them that the takings for the current year were lower than expected. It included figures which matched those kept by Phyllis and were not good reading. It informed them that, as a result, the budget for the following season was to be reduced by 50% and gave notice that, should the figures not improve, the company might close the site although there may be sites elsewhere around the country where warden positions could be applied for.

Phyllis shed a few tears and Reg was quiet too. They had grown to love Camus and had made so many friends. Becoming a warden elsewhere offered no consolation but Reg did not believe in self pity. He was a great believer in positive thought. Fergal was nearly ready to be put back into service. Just the paint job needed to be done and so Reg and Angus spent several more sessions together in the steading carefully painting each part and planning for the future.

FROM SHAW TO SEA

AS OCTOBER APPROACHED, visitor numbers, already low, were rapidly tapering off, leaving Reg with a little more time on his hands.

Fergal was now finished and the site was, as always, in good order. Reg therefore more than welcomed Angus's invitation to go stalking with Niall on the estate. Angus hadn't even held a gun for many years but, should their hunt be successful, Niall would arrange for the venison to be prepared and shared between them. Phyllis wasn't too sure about this at the outset. She ate meat, of course, but never killed anything herself. Reg on the other hand was excited at the prospect of shooting again. After all, it was over ten years since he had last handled a rifle in the army. Angus suggested that they should have a few practice sessions, as they were both a bit rusty, using the Royal Enfield .303, ex army issue rifle, that Angus had been given by his father. Like a pair of schoolboys, they would venture off across the fields to the target which Reg had made in his workshop.

Phyllis could hear the shots from Camus. The smile on Reg's face, each time he returned, went from ear to ear. He didn't mean to gloat but his ability with the rifle was quite remarkable and he easily outscored Angus. He surprised himself at how quickly those skills returned but then, so far, they were aiming at a stationary target.

"What we really need" suggested Reg "is to understand the enemy or should I say stag. Any chance that we could practice the stalking without the rifle?"

So the pair planned a practice run. They packed their sandwiches and dressed in suitably camouflaged clothing, dismissing any suggestion that they looked, in any way, like 'Survival Man'. They set off quite early, telling their respective wives that they might be gone for some time.

Phyllis was left to look after the site and its few remaining guests so she invited Elaine to come and spend some time with her. Elaine could detect that something was up with Phyllis.

"Are you ok hen?" she asked in her soft, soothing accent.

"I can't help worrying about Camus and whether the company might pull the plug on us" she replied. "I feel that we belong here now and I can't bear the thought of leaving".

"Well maybe you won't have to. How many enquiries do you get now from your website?" Elaine asked.

"Quite a few but of course we have to pay 50% of the site fees to the company".

"And how many do you get from the flyers we spread around the area?"

"Not as many. It's probably because most people bringing a caravan here have pre-planned their stay rather than just passing trade."

"Do you keep a record of how they found out about Camus?" asked Elaine.

"Yes they tick a box when they register".

"Lets go through the books and do a bit of detective work then" Elaine suggested. The ladies smiled at each other and immediately set about the task.

For Reg and Angus, stalking a deer presented a challenge all of its own. It was possible to stalk either a stag or hinds until the official start of the rut. Angus might not be top dog as far as the shooting was concerned but he certainly knew more about where and how to look for the 'monarch of the glen', after all the territory was more familiar to him.

They started with a long walk, making their way across the hills to where Angus was convinced they might find what they were after. The glen was beautiful, already showing the early signs of the colours of autumn. This was a truly wild and remote landscape, one in which Reg by now felt at home. Angus told Reg that when they got a little closer they would start 'spying' which apparently is the term used by stalkers to describe identifying the location of the deer. Reg found this highly amusing and was already feeling the adrenaline rush of the hunt. When they had spotted their target, they would need to make progress in a slow and patient approach, taking great care not only to conceal themselves but also stay downwind as these majestic beasts are easily spooked. Should they get close enough to take the imaginary shot they would both be crawling. Reg quickly patted his stomach which was potentially a bit more of an obstacle than it would have been in his army days.

"That's a sign of good living" laughed Angus.

The stalk went as planned. They eventually came to a ridge where they caught sight, in their binoculars, of no less than three stags grazing amongst the heather. They were however a way off so Reg and Angus stayed out of sight, just over the ridge, and made their way gradually closer. Transversing the ridge itself and yet staying out of sight of their targets would be a real test. They crouched and slowly slid their way down into the glen, pausing briefly behind any small shrub they could find. It is well known that deer graze and strip young saplings and that, in an attempt to re-forest some areas, tall fences have to be erected to keep the deer out. Perhaps the deer are conscious of this because many of the glens in which they are found offer little cover for the hunter. Finally they managed to crawl to a position which would have been barely close enough for a good shot, before one stag must have caught their smell and with head alert, he trotted off proudly, encouraging the other two to follow. The objective had however been achieved and they now felt prepared for the stalk itself, less than a week away.

"It's all very well to spot a stag" said Angus "but we also need to be mindful of its condition. We really don't want to shoot a fine healthy beast. Niall will be aware of the older, weaker ones to look for."

Reg was learning that deer stalking in Scotland was an important part of land management, helping to protect native plants and species. It also helps to protect the near chronic over-population of deer. In addition, it is important to the local economy.

Phyllis and Elaine had gone through all the visitor books, preparing a grid with a space for each month of each year that Camus had been operating. Each space was then assigned four sections - one for bookings direct from Touring Haven holidays, another for responses to their own website, another for introduction following their leaflets and an 'other'. Phyllis read out the findings from her registration book whilst Elaine marked the appropriate area of the grid. They made themselves endless cups of tea, thoroughly enjoying their afternoon.

They had just finished marking their chart when the men returned like two naughty schoolboys. They were both covered in mud and grass stains and couldn't wait to tell the ladies all about their day. Elaine and Angus needed to return home to the rest of the family, having agreed that Elaine would take the grid home and return with a proper analysis of their findings.

A week later it was time for the boys' day out. A mist hung in the air which was slow to clear. They headed off to meet Niall, trying hard to contain their excitement. Meanwhile, Elaine returned with a professional-looking document to discuss her findings with Phyllis. She had entered the data they had collected in a spreadsheet, from which she had produced impressive pie charts helping Phyllis to see quickly the analysis of bookings. Surprisingly, the bookings made through Touring Haven holidays started at almost 90% of the visiting vans but, as the seasons progressed, this had gradually dropped, with the season just ending showing only 50% of the bookings through their landlord. Bookings in total had increased from 186 in the first year to 312 last season, only dropping again this year due to the weather. The number of visitors making a booking after visiting the website now accounted for almost 40% of the total. When looking at the trend, it was noticeable that the visiting campers had also increased since the opening of Donnie's kayak venture. Over yet more tea and cakes, Elaine made Phyllis realise that, even if the company should pull out, she and Reg were clearly making a success of Camus and that perhaps it would be possible to run it as a truly independent site.

When the boys eventually returned, having enjoyed a few drammies with Niall, they were still exhilarated by the experience. They had succeeded in shooting a stag which had been taken back to the estate for the venison to be properly checked and prepared. Apparently it was Reg who took the shot, the accuracy of which had become the talk of the estate.

"Here, Niall has offered Reg a part-time job taking rough shooting parties. What do you think of that?" Angus asked the ladies.

They obviously thought he was joking.

"They'd have to get used to taking orders" Phyllis added making a secret dig at her husband. "Still I'm really glad that you enjoyed your day. Will the venison be ready in time to take back to Worcester?"

They returned to Worcester at the start of November, together with the venison. Of course, Reg made sure that their friends were aware of his contribution to the meal. Once again it was a family Christmas but Phyllis's dad was not at all well. He was now 95 and with every passing year he was weaker. Phyllis worried that he might not be able to live on his own much longer. Perhaps if the site did close, she would be back in their bungalow and able to take more care of him. He obviously couldn't come to Camus with them in a caravan. Annie and Craig made regular visits but as Ellie was getting older and now another grandchild was on the way, it was a lot to ask of them.

Between Christmas and the start of February, they repeatedly returned to the same topic of conversation. What did the future hold for them? They had so enjoyed the last four years and neither could bear to see it all come to an end. Apart from Phyllis's dad and the obvious benefit in being closer to take good care of him, they always found themselves longing for those winter months to pass. Having spent nearly all their lives south of the border, they now felt an inexplicable belonging to Scotland's west coast. Phyllis had long discussions with Reg about the prospect of running the site as an independent business if Touring Haven holidays were to withdraw. If the company decided to end their lease, would it be viable for them to continue independently? Still there were more questions than answers and, anyway, they were already determined to up their game the following season and prove to the company that Camus was worth keeping.

It was late February when Henry sadly passed away. He died peacefully in his sleep in his own home and Phyllis, although grieving, took great consolation from that. She so wished that he had been able to come to Camus but, instead, he had had to take pleasure from the photographs they always brought back with them. The funeral was a quiet affair but

Phyllis was particularly touched by the attendance of Meg who, although she had only met Henry the previous Christmas, had made the long journey to support her friend.

There was much to sort out once the funeral had passed. They would normally have returned to Camus in early March but, as Phyllis was the only child, it was left to her to sort out her father's estate. From speaking to Meg and Angus on the phone, it was just as well that they had been detained in Worcester as a significant amount of snow was continuing to plague the west coast. It was not unusual for wintry conditions to come with a vengeance in February but this year the bitter cold was continuing long into March. Angus told Reg that, as much of the ground was still blanketed in snow, there was little he could be doing preparing for the start of the season in April. They therefore left their journey until the last minute. Angus had kindly checked that the plumbing was all intact and that no pipes were frozen, although much of this was down to the extra lagging that Reg had put in place as insurance against such a harsh winter. They need not have rushed to the site as the roads were still treacherous and there was little prospect of any caravans arriving for the start of the official season. A few bookings which had been made were soon cancelled. Not the start they had hoped for.

This was the first snow that Reg and Phyllis had seen and in spite of the obvious detriment to visitors, Camus was strangely beautiful. Snow on the west coast was quite rare. The skies were clear and blue and yet the temperature was still zero degrees or below which, meant that the snow cover was slow to thaw and the ground was as hard as nails. Reg and Phyllis's van was reputed to be good for temperatures as low as -15c but they had to admit that for the first time they actually felt cold. The snow rendered the hills and glens even quieter than before and when Reg went out for his regular walks he could hear the distant barking of the stags high up in the mountains. Many of the small burns were still frozen solid. The burn running under the hump backed bridge was still flowing but ice crystals sparkled on the water's edge.

Easter was late this year with school holidays not starting until the second week of April but it wasn't until mid-April that marsh marigold and the heather started to show their colours. Visitors, too, were cautiously slow to arrive resulting in only a total of six vans throughout the Easter period.

Reg was pleased to see that three of his bird boxes were in various stages of occupation. Some blue tits were busily taking moss and heather in to one, clearly nest-building. Another had been claimed by a pair of coal tits, who appeared to have finished building their nest and were taking turns to incubate the eggs. The third box was a real first for Reg as it had attracted a pair of crested tits, not seen south of the border. Their crazy punk-style head feathers made them a particular pleasure to watch through his binoculars. Indeed, crested tits were not common to Camus and are protected. They can only usually be found in the old Scots pine forests further north east but this pair had obviously strayed, probably from the forest just across the fields. The boxes were all placed on trees towards the edge of the site but occasionally the birds were enticed to the bird table outside the reception, where Phyllis was in charge of maintaining a complete array of feeders offering nuts, niger seed, meal worms, fat balls and juicy dangling coconuts.

Visitors loved to watch the seemingly endless arrivals and several had mentioned it in the comments in their visitor book. Reg had also positioned a covered bird table at the edge of the site, allowing more secluded feeding for the nesting birds. It was further away from the reception and caravans but it was obviously well used, judging by the number of times that Phyllis had to fill the now empty containers. It was when Phyllis was making her early morning visit to replenish the feeders that she saw a cute, red squirrel happily sitting on the bird table enjoying a mouthful of nuts. Although she was aware that the nearby forest was a favourite haunt of the reds, she had rarely seen many. She stopped some distance away. He or she was instantly recognisable not only by the russet coloured fur but also by the enchanting tufted ears, beautiful white tummy and long fluffy tail. Although she and Reg had now been at Camus for over four years she still didn't think to have her camera at hand in spite of the fact that, almost daily, there was always something magical to be seen around the site. No wonder that the nut feeder was emptied almost every other day but Phyllis didn't mind; she felt privileged to have such a visitor and hoped that she might see him or her another morning.

By June the bookings were increasing, particularly those secured through their own website. June was also seeing Phyllis's baskets blossoming impressively. By now she had got Reg to make more troughs, which completely surrounded the reception and their own van too. The shower block now had a full display of hanging baskets, with begonias in shades of pink, yellow, red white and orange. When they reached their peak in July, the flowers were larger than ever and this year

Phyllis had included Dichondra Silver Falls which, not only provided a beautiful contrast with its training green and silver stems but also afforded a protection to the brightly coloured flowers when the winds picked up.

They had some memorable guests through those summer months. The Broon family came bringing with them a small, insignificant but endlessly energetic Jack Russell. His name was Jake but Reg and Phyllis referred to him as Houdini owing to his ability to wriggle repeatedly out of his collar and lead, spreading disaster and panic across the whole site. The Broon children were also small, probably both under seven, but they too raced around with boundless energy, often chasing Houdini on his frequent escapes. Phyllis wondered whether the whole family's diet consisted of foods loaded with E- numbers but, whatever the reason, their visit certainly left its mark.

Mornings generally on Camus were relaxed and casual, with visitors waking at various times and setting up their tables ready for breakfast. Toast and cereal were common but some visitors even prepared a full English cooked affair, either in their van or on camping stoves carefully erected outside. Houdini just couldn't resist the temptation to check out as many tables as possible. With minimal effort, he prized himself from his lead, which was staked in the ground, and raced about at speed for fear that the children might soon be sent to retrieve him. Phyllis heard the commotion from inside the reception and when she ventured out she could see the whirlwind dog racing in and out of people's vans, awnings, even tents, quickly pursued by a host of angry guests. Several had had their tables upset by the pesky invader and Mr and

Mrs Knowles were particularly angry about the loss of two of their sausages, which were in the process of cooking.

Reg made a series of visits to the Broons to request that Jake was kept on a lead at all times. He had even suggested to them that they might have to leave him locked in their car to minimise the impact on others. These suggestions were always accepted but Jake defied all efforts to restrict his mission of destruction. One day he caught sight of Norman peacefully chewing the cud in the field next to the site. His urge to play compelled him to escape, once again and sprint under the fence in the hope that Norman might enjoy a game of chase. Had the field been full of sheep and lambs, Jake's enthusiasm might have ended in disaster but Norman was fortunately not scared by this miniscule, noisy upstart. After several minutes of repeated racing between his legs and jumping to grab his tail, Norman did, however, become uncharacteristically irritated and let out a serious grunt, which, at least, resulted in Jake turning tail to head back to the site.

As if the complaints were not enough for Reg and Phyllis to cope with, the final straw came when Jake found an old piece of fishing net down on the beach. What a marvellous toy to pull around and engage the children in frequent games of tug! The best game of all was to duck and dive around the site with Jake flicking his head from side to side, complete with the rapidly fraying net in his mouth, pursued by the children trying to extract it from him. It was during one such game that the trio's chase completely encircled the reception. Phyllis felt like a cowboy trapped inside by Indians when her attention was focused on a series of coloured petals briefly rising up to the window before slowly drifting back to the ground. She rushed outside clapping her hands to shoo the dog and the children away but the damage had already been done. Jake had dragged his net across and in between her prize troughs, resulting in serious damage to the previously beautiful displays. She could have cried and Reg had decided that enough was enough.

He went back once again to the Broon's van, having succeeded in catching Houdini and restraining him under his arm. This time he insisted that, as they only had one more day to go, Jake must be shut in the car at all times and that any more walks must be taken off site. Mrs Broon did come to apologise most sincerely to Phyllis and offered to pay for the damage but, by now, it was too late to replant the troughs and Phyllis simply had to do her best to remove the damaged flowers and tidy up as best she could.

Then, of course, there was the noteworthy visit from the unusually large Mrs Shaw. Phyllis assumed that Mrs Shaw must have been travelling for some time, judging by the amount of washing she pegged out on a hastily improvised line erected between two poles staked into the ground by Mr Shaw. They had chosen a front pitch ensuring that the clothes benefited from the fresh sea breeze. Reg was somewhat perturbed by the interruption to the normally spectacular view afforded to all their guests but they were such a bubbly couple he simply hoped that the intrusion of their laundry would quickly pass.

Angus found the whole episode very entertaining. He simply couldn't believe the size of the knickers which he envisaged would be sufficient to act as a sail and power his boat if it were not for the onboard motor. Phyllis told him off for fear that Mrs Shaw might be embarrassed had she realised the source of his amusement. Having filled their line, the Shaws then left for the day, intending to visit the lighthouse.

"Well" said Angus "They need not have bothered to build it all those years ago if they'd seen her bloomers hung out to dry. They would be sure to ward off any sailors venturing too close".

Reg nearly choked on his coffee and Phyllis gave him a slap on his arm.

"Don't be so cruel" remarked Phyllis although she too was displaying a crack in her stern face.

During the day the wind was picking up and Phyllis was starting to wonder whether she should collect and neatly fold the garments which, by now, were surely completely dry. She didn't want to interfere but was worried by the fact that some items had already dislodged a peg or two. She should have acted sooner because just as she was watching the flailing garments from her window, one of Mrs Shaw's bras was snatched from the line, whisked in to the air and headed out in the direction of the sea. Her brassieres too, it must be said, were an appropriate match to her knickers. Phyllis thought that they must be a least a size 50FF although Angus thought that considering his own XXXL measurement she must surely be off the Richter scale!!

The breeze had taken the bra a fair way out and then dropped it on to the water. Reg used his binoculars and soon realised that it must have landed trapping air inside the enormous cups thus leaving it floating helplessly on the surface. Poor Mrs Shaw - if only Phyllis had acted sooner. Nevertheless she was just about to venture out to collect all the remaining items when an unexpected 4x4 pulled up at reception. It was a gentleman from Touring Haven Holidays who was paying a surprise visit to check out the site. With him came another man, equipped with a clipboard and a camera.

He introduced himself as Bob and handed a business card to Reg. The two men were simply passing and thought that they would find out how everything was going. Reg did not appreciate being treated as if he were simple. There was no way that they had arrived by chance and he was therefore particularly guarded with his answers.

"We're fine" he said "keeping busy looking after our visitors". Unfortunately though the site was not at its best. Mrs Shaw's garments were flapping about and the normally impressive flower troughs were bearing the scars inflicted by Houdini. As always though the reception, toilets and sheds were immaculate and at least there were a good dozen vans currently on site.

"You don't mind if we just have a look around do you?" asked the other smartly dressed man.

"No by all means. Shall I come with you?" Reg asked thinking that he might get more of an indication as to the real reason for their visit.

"No, we'll be just fine" said Bob as the two men headed off across the site.

They were there walking about for quite some time. Reg and Phyllis retired to their van from where they could get a clear view of what the pair were up to. They were clearly taking notes on their clipboard and a series of photos.

"I reckon they're going to sell up" said Reg observing the worried look on Phyllis's face. "I suppose that we'll find out eventually".

"There's normally more vans than this" remarked Phyllis "We've got 20 booked for next week."

Before the pair left they came in to reception and asked to see the visitor details for this season. It wasn't impressive reading. When they had gone Phyllis checked the figures, making herself thoroughly depressed.

"Don't worry about it" said Reg putting his arm around her. "You know me dear, forever the optimist. Perhaps some good may come of this after all."

Later that afternoon Mrs Shaw returned and Phyllis made her way towards their van with the sadly depleted clothes, now dried and neatly folded. She explained to Mrs Shaw that the wind had got stronger during the day so she had taken it upon herself to take the washing from the line. Unfortunately though, one of the items had already blown out to sea and Phyllis hoped that she would manage without it. Of course she didn't specify which article of clothing had been lost, respecting Mrs Shaw's modesty, but by the next morning, when the sea was like a mill pond beautifully calm and tranquil, it soon became obvious to everyone when the spectacle of twin peaks bobbed about unashamedly all the following day.

THE ANIMALS' CHANCE
OF STARDOM

IMPRESSED BY REG'S ability with the rifle, Niall had agreed to ask Reg to assist with both rough shooting parties and clay pigeon shooting on the estate. The term 'rough shooting' is not in any way a poor relation to stalking, indeed it is very popular, often with 'well to do' visitors to the estate who frequently find a snipe, a woodcock or at least a rabbit. Reg had put up a poster in the reception advertising the clay pigeon shooting which was attracting attention from some of his guests at Camus. Not only was he himself a good shot but he was used to instructing others, which made him a popular choice as a coach. Although the people taking part had paid for their opportunity, it was not unusual, particularly with the rough shooting, for Reg to return with a tip, sometimes up to £50. On average he took a group for a few hours twice a week. It was not as if he needed extra money but more about keeping the old skills alive.

Ironically the weather was particularly fine from late September onwards and Camus was busy for that part of the season. Several wise, retired guests looked forward to the disappearance of the midges before venturing out themselves. This year an older couple arrived, Mr and Mrs Cooper from Aberdeen. They chose a pitch looking out to sea and Mrs Cooper could be seen levelling the van, connecting to the hook-up, filling the aqua roll and generally doing all the tasks which were normally either shared or for the most part undertaken by the men. Mr Cooper however seemed to be totally engrossed in setting up a brand new satellite dish. He started by opening the box and puzzling over the wires and other parts inside. His wife was now unloading the picnic chairs from the boot of their car, which was just as well as Mr Cooper now had somewhere comfortable to sit whilst he was reading the instruction booklet.

Phyllis was staring from her window in disbelief. Reg had always been very chivalrous through their 34 years of marriage. Never had she been left to do all the work while Reg sat down doing his own thing. She assumed that the process of setting up this dish was not going smoothly as Mr Cooper had moved it around the pitch from one location to another. He was obviously communicating with his wife, now inside her van, presumably seeking confirmation regarding the picture quality as he moved the dish around outside. Goodness knows what her responses were but they must have been negative as his manoeuvres continued for at least 15 minutes. Eventually she emerged with a cup of tea in hand and sat herself down outside to enjoy the breathtaking view. Mr Cooper however was totally focused on getting the best signal. There must surely be something important he wanted to watch.

Reg and Phyllis never failed to be amused by the lengths people seem to go to get their TVs working. For them the TV went on each evening for the news and weather but, other than a few select programmes, they rarely sat down to watch. There was invariably something far more interesting to observe outside. After a while, two other male guests joined Mr Cooper admiring his brand new purchase and, no doubt, offering advice as all three of them were soon on the case. Mr Cooper went inside to check the picture while one of the other two gents took over the repositioning and the third was turning the pages of the instruction book. Finally they must have achieved their objective as all three men disappeared into the van, leaving Mrs Cooper outside on her own.

After a while she made her way towards the reception, giving Phyllis the chance to talk.

"Did they get it sorted in the end?" she asked politely.

"I presume so" Mrs Cooper sighed despairingly "He makes me so mad though. We almost didn't come until tomorrow so that he wouldn't miss the match."

"Oh you're a football widow" Phyllis smiled.

"They're all the same. I suppose your husband is glued to it as well."

"No, he doesn't like football" replied Phyllis "He's a rugby man but he rarely sits and watches the telly anyway".

"Then he must be a rare breed" Mrs Cooper said somewhat resentfully. She had come to choose a few postcards but also to see the visitor display board and pick up some leaflets on local attractions.

"Would you like me to show you around?" asked Phyllis, sensing her feeling of isolation.

"Yes that would be nice, thank you" she replied. The two ladies strolled around the site, with Phyllis pointing out the various facilities and taking Mrs Cooper down the slipway to the beach. She said her name was Jean and that she too enjoyed her tubs and hanging baskets, which kept the ladies discussing their favourites and tips, relating to containers, for some considerable time. Phyllis felt the need to apologise for the sad state of her troughs courtesy of Houdini, the troublesome canine visitor several weeks prior. Jean revealed that she and her husband came from a small hamlet a few miles from Aberdeen and that they had visited the west coast several times previously but never as far as Camus. She had used the internet to trace her family tree only to find that her great-grandmother came from one of the small isles, which she was therefore keen to visit. Jean believed that the island was called Ulva. Phyllis immediately suggested that she should see Jimmy at the ferry just a few miles along the coast. He ran a trip to Ulva every Wednesday.

Mr Cooper and his newly found friends were still ensconced in front of the telly when the ladies returned to the van. Phyllis and Jean were so busy chatting that Jean failed to look at the trailing lead from the satellite dish, which she unfortunately tripped over, pulling the lead from the dish and landing heavily on her shoulder. Phyllis was really concerned as Jean let out a painful scream which was more than matched by Mr Cooper's expletive which came from inside the van. He poked his head out, already starting to shout at her. Phyllis wasn't sure whether it was her presence, or the sight of his wife lying face down in obvious pain, that lead to his change of plan but either way he quickly made his way to help her to the chair. He asked if she was ok and then immediately reconnected the lead and left her in Phyllis's care whilst he returned swiftly to enjoy the remainder of the game.

Had that been Reg, he would have stopped everything to make sure that Phyllis was alright. He would have showed more concern, made her comfortable and then offered to make her some tea. In the absence of any such attention, Phyllis invited Jean back to her van for a soothing warm drink. They didn't normally invite guests to their van but Phyllis was so angry at Mr Cooper's lack of priority that she decided to make Jean an exception.

Her arm was clearly causing her a lot of pain so Reg was called to help. He had first aid training and soon supported her arm in a professionally made sling for which she was extremely grateful. Clearly the game must have finished because Mr Cooper appeared sheepishly at the door of their van. When he saw his wife with her arm in a sling he showed an embarrassed concern.

"I didn't realise that you were hurt dear" he said.

"I've checked" snapped Reg "I don't think that anything's broken but we've put on a sling as she was quite uncomfortable. That should give her a bit more support". He placed particular emphasis on the word 'support'.

Mr Cooper thanked them both for their help and hurriedly encouraged his wife back to their van, offering his hand to assist her down the step. Jean, too, thanked them both for their kindness.

"Good job you were both there" she said, as if to shame her husband even more. "Oh and thanks for the suggestions about the ferry. I'll be sure to follow that up."

"That man's something else!" said Phyllis as soon as they were out of earshot. "Fancy coming here and worrying more about the TV than your wife's predicament".

Jean did exactly as Phyllis suggested and visited the ferry boathouse booking a trip to Ulva. She had heard so much about it from her grandmother when she was just a child. According to stories, told to her by her parents it was beautiful, just like a tropical island. Jean just had to go and visit. In one respect her great-grandmother was right. It was beautiful although hardly as warm as a tropical island indeed it rained for most of their trip. Jean and her husband spent several hours on Ulva without seeing another soul. Although she felt pleased to have seen it she also felt very sad. Ulva was now so empty with only a few inhabitants and it left Jean deeply moved. So many folk and been forced away effectively displaced and dispossessed. She would certainly look more in to its history when she returned home.

Reg and Phyllis had certainly experienced all types since welcoming their guests to Camus over the last five years. The young, the old, couples and families, campers, caravanners, motor homes, the posh, the not-so-particular, the knowledgeable and the eccentric. They had seen arguments and laughter and at times guests who were showing all the signs of a few too many.

They would never forget the Miltons, who came with a seemingly endless supply of alcohol. Had Camus been on the Hebridean island of Barra, it might have been conceivable that they had stumbled upon a few left over supplies from the SS Politician, famous, of course, for the story of 'Whisky Galore'. However Camus was miles from Barra and they were too far away for any to have been uncovered here. They had a very old van and every evening they could be seen staggering between their van and the toilet block, often covering twice the distance that it would take them during the day.

On several evenings Reg would do his usual round as darkness fell, only to find either Mr or Mrs Milton slumped in a heap in a corner of the site. Many a time he helped them back to their van as they fell through the door. During the day they were like all the other guests, bright and chirpy and going about their business but as evening fell they retired to their van for more than a few drammies. Unfortunately however, on one particular evening Mrs Milton inadvertently returned from the toilet and let herself into a very smart caravan. How she had mistaken it for her own tired van clearly showed the lack of judgement brought on by yet another over-indulgence. The unsuspecting couple, already tucked up in their plush, fixed bed, got up and tried to help her out but as she fell to the ground they felt that they had no option but to escort her home. Fortunately they recognised her from a brief hello earlier in the day so they knew which van she belonged to. Decked in their pyjamas, they tapped on the door of the van but there was no reply, simply a heavy snoring indicating that Mr Milton was indeed inside. They managed to get Mrs Milton inside the door but she simply collapsed across the bed made up in the lounge. Neither of them wanted to go inside not knowing whether the snoring Mr Milton was pleased to have his wife returned or whether he was even aware that she had gone.

The next day the rescuing couple went to the office to ask whether the lady was ok giving Phyllis the full details of the incident. Unbelievably Mrs Milton appeared to buy the morning's milk, obviously totally oblivious to the events of the previous night. She greeted them all with her usual smile and wished them all a nice day.

"He's done it again" she said "too much to drink last night and now sleeping like a baby."

Towards the end of what was Reg and Phyllis's fifth season the dreaded letter from Touring Haven Holidays arrived. It was sympathetically worded, confirming that Camus was not meeting the expected returns of the company and that, after much consideration by the Board; it had been decided not to continue trading in the following year. The letter thanked them for all their hard work and advised them that, if they wished to move as wardens of another site, they would be automatically offered any positions which became available. The site would therefore close on 31st October.

The trouble was that neither Reg nor Phyllis felt that they were ready to move on. Although they had been here for five seasons now, they had so many ideas they still wanted to explore. This was further re-enforced when Meg was asked to make a booking for four TV presenters who were planning to make a short series about the autumn wildlife in Scotland. They were planning to come at the very end of October and intended to bring a number of motor homes and lorries containing the entire camera and recording equipment. Meg had suggested that they would be able to park up at Camus and gave them Reg's mobile number.

From the moment the letter arrived in late September, there was little else that was the topic of local conversation. Elaine, Angus, Meg and Niall were all insistent that Reg and Phyllis should stay on. The TV crew were due to arrive at the very end of October and stay through most of November. They had allowed the first week to check out the whole area and a further three weeks to get the necessary footage. The trouble was that Reg and Phyllis would no longer be wardens from 1st November. However, as Hamish's solicitor had received notice of the surrender of the lease, Angus had already agreed with his father that, in return for a small fee, they could stay and accept the booking from the TV crew independently. Phyllis felt relieved that she did not need to return to Worcester as early as expected and Reg made plans to prepare their caravan for the start of winter. They were both quite overwhelmed by the excitement that this turn of events had precipitated in all their neighbours and indeed throughout the local community.

Much discussion ensued between Reg, Phyllis, Angus and Elaine from that point on, with Elaine relentlessly urging Phyllis to continue at Camus for at least another full season. They were all encouraged by the TV coverage and resulting free advertising that the series would offer. Angus was keen for Donnie to promote his kayak trips and Reg had agreed that a refurbishment of the toilet block was in order if they were to stay for another season.

The TV crew were to bring four lorries, containing all their recording equipment, and a large motor home to house the technicians. Meg was to accommodate the two presenters, producer and editor. The crew were prepared to pay a reasonable fee for their use of the site but Reg was quick to negotiate a good deal for their stay, which included copies of some of the wildlife pictures they captured and photos of the presenters, both on the site and at Meg's B&B which they would be allowed to display on their web site.

Reg had planned that the toilet block refurb would take two weeks involving incorporating a third shower cubicle in both the ladies' and the men's, new tiling for the walls, a fresh coat of paint and new shower curtains and Phyllis was keen to go shopping again and choose the appropriate colour schemes. Somehow they undertook these tasks with renewed enthusiasm; already assuming that their hard work would not only be of benefit to the TV crew but potentially to another season of 'their own' guests.

Reg's opportunity to assist Niall with shooting parties was extended but he was conscious of the need to complete the refurbishment before October was out, so he had to share his time between these commitments. Angus lent a hand whenever he could and the two men discussed plans for the following season. Donnie's kayaking business had attracted an increase in campers; perhaps they should consider converting the steading in to a bunkhouse to afford the campers a place to escape the ravages of the wind and rain which so often left them and their clothes drenched.

Phyllis spent a lot of time with Elaine looking at every opportunity to market the site more widely. Firstly they edited the leaflets incorporating details of Donnie's business, including tariffs and a booking telephone number. They sent leaflets and details of their website to several companies who specialised in the hire of motor homes, particularly popular in this part of Scotland. Elaine hastily printed vouchers entitling the hirers to a free night at Camus whenever they booked a total of three nights. They telephoned each of the companies to establish a contact and sent them a decent supply of brochures.

October passed by only too quickly, with the last few guests gradually dwindling away. Fortunately the TV crew were all men, apart from one of the presenters who had booked to stay at Meg's. That meant that Reg could refurb the ladies' shower block first, leaving the men's in clean working order. When the ladies' was finished, the TV crew could swap over albeit that Phyllis would use the blue shower curtains rather than the lilac ones she had chosen eventually for the ladies!

There were six young guys, operating all the camera and other technical equipment. Reg had found out what power supply they would require and had made sure that they had the necessary supply of armoured cable, which could run directly from his workshop as the pitch hook-up points were clearly inadequate. Phyllis had enquired before they arrived regarding their requirements for bread, milk and other provisions and had placed the orders to ensure that they would have everything they needed.

The director and producer had paid an unannounced visit to Meg several weeks prior and had already planned what they hoped to film. Their intention was to film pine martens who could regularly be seen in the Caledonian pine trees in Meg's garden and who had clearly learned that the scraps placed occasionally on the table by Meg were a delicacy not to be missed. They were also planning to stalk on the estate with Niall, not to kill, but to get footage of the stags in the rutting season. They were particularly interested in the reports of an otter at Camus and had planned to set up remote control cameras along the shore close to the slipway. The opportunities for birds were too numerous to mention but the local rumours that there had been a Scottish wild cat in the area had the researchers particularly excited.

Talking of excitement it was inconceivable to exclude Norman from the proceedings. When the TV crew arrived with four loaded lorries and an impressive motor home, he could not miss this irresistible opportunity for stardom. He set himself up in prime position on the bridge, with absolutely no intention of moving. He stood there, head held high with his long horns seeming to present a complete barricade across the width of the bridge. His thick downy undercoat had just started to grow back in anticipation of the fast approaching winter, whilst his long, well oiled, red outer coat endured, providing all-round protection from the wind, rain and insects. If only he had resisted the temptation to poke out his tongue, curling it up and covering his top lip, he might have looked more menacing but there was surely a photo opportunity coming up. However it was Norman who was in for a surprise when two of the crew jumped out of the first lorry. One was holding an impressively long camera which made a series of repeated clicks for longer than Norman was accustomed to. Reg was already approaching; pellets to the ready; mind you, today Norman seemed to require more of an incentive to move than the usual, simple lure of food. By now Reg was used to moving him out of the way with a simple tap on the backside and, to use Meg's words, a stern instruction of 'Tar, Tormad'. As soon as Reg had encouraged him to stand aside, the large vehicles moved towards the site with Norman following curiously.

Meg had kindly prepared a large pot of stovies which she had already told them to expect after their long journey. She was due to arrive, at Camus, later that evening. She had also prepared a smaller pot for herself, Reg and Phyllis to share in their caravan. Fortunately it was a fine afternoon, although the light was already fading by 3 o'clock so the crew were keen to take a tour of the site before then. They admired the views and strolled down to the slipway where they were to set up remote cameras the following morning. They also thought that positioning a camera inside the steading might afford them some footage of the barn owl. When they spotted the burn heading down the side of the site from under 'Norman's' bridge, they seemed particularly captivated. Reg thought back to his childhood and how he had enjoyed 'Tales of the Riverbank' which had clearly inspired camera crews many years ago.

Phyllis had made them a welcoming pot of tea which they all shared inside their rather plush motor home. All six of them could comfortably sleep inside - two above the bulk head and four more in bunk beds situated at the rear. After their tea and tour around the site, Reg and Phyllis left them in peace to settle in. They were already looking forward to acting as hosts to such a nice people for the next four weeks.

Meg duly arrived with the promised stovies which Reg and Phyllis had already assured the crew would not disappoint. Her four B&B guests were not due to arrive until the end of the week so Phyllis had agreed to help her get all the necessary provisions from the mainland. Of course, the meat and dairy produce was sourced locally and special orders had been placed with Joyce to prepare the best crab for later in their stay.

EVERYONE LOVES A CEILIDH

THE NEXT MORNING everyone was up early. The TV guys were obviously well used to early starts. By the inviting smell coming from the motor home, they were starting the day with bacon rolls having ordered three dozen a day, immensely pleasing the local baker. Phyllis thought that it would be impolite not to familiarise herself with their names but knowing that she wasn't good at remembering names she took a note pad with her to keep for future reference.

The one who appeared to be in charge was Chris. Phyllis made a note that he had long hair tied back in a pony tail. Richard was the technical whiz kid responsible for setting up all of the remote cameras and monitoring screens. He was easy to remember as he was completely bald and somewhat round. Michael was the youngest. Phyllis thought that he was more like a trainee, especially when she noted that he did most of the cooking and was often sent off to make the tea. Jonathon was the real hive of all knowledge, always called upon by the others in the team to provide specific advice regarding the animals themselves. He had an Irish accent and Phyllis thought that he was particularly handsome. The last two were Ben and Stephen. Ben had distinct sideburns and Stephen a mass of curly hair, which Phyllis duly noted in her book.

Donnie was more than happy to help the team out by providing four wheel drive transport from the site. It was nice for him to spend time with other young men who shared a passion for the outdoors. He had already been communicating with Jonathon by e-mail having been given his contact details by Meg and, as agreed, Donnie took him out to the cliffs near to the Ardnamurchan Point Lighthouse where there was a long-established golden eagle nest.

Angus and Donnie had seen the pair of eagles many times from Angus's boat whilst out at sea tending their creels. As eagles are monogamous, pairing for life, it was almost certainly the same adults who had occupied the nesting area all year. They had a series of similar nests along that stretch of coast, each one being a large structure of branches, twigs and heather, something between one and one and a half meters wide. Unusually this year there were two juveniles who would normally have been driven away by the adults come October but this year, even as November was fast approaching, they were still returning to the nest, clearly enjoying the home comforts. Jonathon was keen to see the nest and weigh up the best position for some good camera shots.

Michael and Ben spent most of the day surveying the burn and its banks. They took with them endless pieces of equipment, returning periodically to check the monitors already fired up by Richard in one of the lorries. They seemed to be talking to him by way of hand-held radios, avoiding the signal problems experienced by many mobile phones. Reg couldn't begin to imagine the likely cost of all this equipment. He had long been a lover of any natural history programmes on TV but was now able to see for himself what was involved. Chris and Stephen had spent a short time near the boathouse but had an appointment at Meg's to check out her garden and the opportunities to film the pine martens.

That evening the lads borrowed Reg's Jeep to visit the Dobhran for a good meal and a beer.

As the week went on, they all worked tirelessly setting up cameras along the shoreline, in the steading, along the burn, suspended from the cliff edge and of course in Meg's garden. Each evening Reg and Phyllis were invited to see what progress was being made. However filming wildlife was by no means guaranteed; apparently over the first three days they had only had minimal success with a few shots of the elusive pine marten feeding off Meg's bird table and three visits to the impressive cliffside eyrie by the juveniles and female eagle. This was not unusual however as it was necessary for the wildlife to settle back alongside these foreign camera objects and the trampled vegetation caused by the activity of the camera crew.

As the days went by, they had managed to capture beautiful shots of the red squirrels visiting Phyllis's table, a cute, gorgeous bank vole who regularly scoured the sides of the burn, carrying off any food it might find, and captivating shots of the barn owl, both leaving the steading and sleeping peacefully inside. On their remote cameras they caught images of the Camus otter scurrying across the slipway, sliding gracefully into the water and returning with whatever crustaceans he was able to collect. Towards the end of the week they had awarded themselves a day off and headed off to the mainland to restock their larder and their reserve of beer.

The director and producer arrived at Meg's in the middle of the following week and confirmed that the two presenters would arrive by 10th November. Again they were youngish and extremely articulate. The director was Tom, who Phyllis assumed was about 45, and the producer was Ed, probably in his early 40's. They first visited the crew at Camus to see what shots they had already captured and to generally check on the progress. Included in their itinerary was a visit to the estate to go through the plans with Niall regarding the filming. They also paid a surprise visit to Angus to ask whether they could accompany him on his boat and follow the progress as he brought in his lobsters. Angus was more than happy to take a few of the crew on board. It was to be Chris, Jonathon and Stephen who would go with him but Angus suggested that they wait for a nice calm evening which would afford easier filming.

The sightings of the wildcat reported by the locals were all further inland where the cover of trees and gorse provided suitable habitat for this elusive animal. The crew set up a hide leaving Michael to report back if anything was spotted. However Michael had surely drawn the short straw as the wildcat is the probably the most endangered species in Britain and has rarely been spotted by even the most determined wildlife researcher.

The two presenters, Julia and Matt, duly arrived and were introduced to all the neighbours. They were both 30-ish. They were inquisitive and approachable and Matt, in particular, had an infectious sense of humour. This was evident when they, together with the rest of the crew, sneaked up to the hide in which Michael was positioned and started to make a faint hissing and growling sound just outside the camouflaged canvass on the opposite side to the opening. When this resulted in no reaction from inside the tent, they all burst in, waking the sleeping Michael and proceeding to tell him that they had captured the most amazing wild cat film footage ever and, having seen it on their monitors back in the lorry, they had rushed out to congratulate him. Having been woken so suddenly, it took Michael some time to realise that they were indeed having him on but for the rest of their stay they prodded him at every conceivable opportunity just to make sure he was awake. After only a few days, the team gave up on their attempt to spot a wildcat and agreed to focus more on the animals who offered a greater chance of being caught on camera.

Whilst the presence of the crew kept Reg fairly busy, there was still time to consider when he and Phyllis might return to Worcester and what they would need if they were to continue for another season. It was already feeling colder in the caravan and they had therefore planned to return to their bungalow before November was out. Ellie was really looking forward to her grandparents returning for Christmas. Their new grandson had arrived in the middle of July but apart from a quick weekend visit, which Phyllis made by train, they had not had a real chance to see him. He had been named

William Henry after his great-grandfather. Of course they received regular photos but he was changing so quickly and they felt that they were surely missing out. Ellie had now been at school for over two years and so wanted to show her Nan how well she could read, draw and add up. She had painted a picture of Angus's boat which she was desperate to show them.

They had, of course, intended to return as soon as the regular season finished but the plans had obviously radically changed since September. They had explained to Annie and Craig that their return had been delayed, due to the arrival of the TV crew but they had not yet told them that they were almost certainly going to return for yet another year.

When the filming was over, Reg quickly shut down the site, storing everything away in the sheds. Phyllis had already packed her suitcase. Somehow the desire to see the family and the knowledge that they would return in another three months made the leaving easier than before.

Meg was due to have her children visit for Christmas which was now only four weeks away. She had two boys, Lewis and Finlay. Lewis was an insurance assessor and Finlay a police officer. Neither was married and they both worked in Glasgow. For once Finlay was given the Christmas week off, which meant that this was to be the first time in several years that they would all be together.

Before the crew bade their farewells they all gathered at Angus's for a party. Elaine and Meg together had prepared a scrumptious buffet with haggis bites, crowdie, miniature scotch pies, smoked salmon and cold venison. They had filled an enormous trifle bowl with Cranachan, a traditional Scots dessert made with oatmeal, raspberries, cream and, of course, whisky. Meg had also baked some of her lovely, melt-in-the-mouth shortbread. To top it all they had arranged for the local Ceilidh band to come and play some traditional music. The band played the bagpipes and the accordion, filling the lounge with tunes such as The Gay Gordons and The Dashing White Seargent. Meg tried desperately to issue dancing instructions to the TV crew and also to Reg and Phyllis but clearly they still had much to learn. The evening was a riot of laughter and enjoyed by everyone.

Although the crew had a lot to do editing the hours of film clips they had taken, they promised to return in the spring to show the programme in the school hall. They had captured the barn owl high up in the steading. According to Jonathon the Latin name for a barn owl is Tyto alba which, considering that 'alba' is the Gaelic name for Scotland, could well become a significant feature of the programme. Camran and Paige were especially excited at the thought that the film would be shown in their school. They couldn't wait to tell their classmates from all around.

Reg and Phyllis's Worcestershire bungalow felt beautifully warm and cosy since Annie had paid a surprise visit and had not only turned on the heating but Craig had spent hours tidying the garden, clearing up the autumn leaves which had long started to fall. It was evening when they finally arrived home. Phyllis was so looking forward to seeing them all and having that long awaited cuddle with her new grandson, William. She opened her fridge to put in the large piece of Aberdeen Angus beef she had brought with her for Sunday's dinner only to find that Annie had prepared a wonderful chocolate trifle, bought milk, cheese and eggs and also in the cupboard was a lovely fresh loaf. She really appreciated her daughter's thoughtfulness and immediately started to feel guilty that she had not shared, with her their intention to return to Camus next March.

Sunday dinner was very special. Ellie loved having her Nan back and longed to hear more stories about Norman. Little William was now four months old and Annie had a huge amount of photos to show them. Ellie was so good with her little brother and loved to bounce around the room making him laugh. He was just about sitting up, propped up by cushions, but his endless chuckles tipped him off balance and he fell harmlessly back on to the carpet.

Ellie's picture of Angus's boat was very good. She had copied the red and yellow colours from the photos they had taken whilst on holiday and cleverly painted two little seals in the water.

"Can we come back again this year?" she asked excitedly.

"Well if Mummy and Daddy say yes then of course you can poppet" replied Phyllis.

"Do I take it that you plan to go back to Camus?" asked Craig already pre-empting the answer.

"Well a lot has happened in the past few weeks" said Reg. "Let's make some tea and tell you all about it."

Annie and Craig already knew that Touring Haven Holidays had pulled out but they had not realised how much local support Reg and Phyllis had been given to persuade them to continue for another year running the site independently. Whilst they would be pleased to see them return to Worcester, they knew how happy their parents had been running the site and how many friends they had made.

Reg talked about the plans he had to convert the steading and how Donnie's kayak business had opened up new opportunities. Phyllis felt that once the TV programme was aired on telly the visitor numbers would be expected to increase significantly. Reg was obviously now well into the rough shooting on the estate and the marketing they had been undertaking in conjunction with Elaine was sure to result in yet more success. Their plans for the following season were clearly mapped out. Henry's bungalow had been sold and with the inheritance Phyllis would use some of the money to do up the steading.

When Ryan, their son, was on a weekend visit just before Christmas, he picked up on their enthusiasm, even suggesting that they could consider investing in some camping pods which would be sure to appeal to those who like the thought of camping but prefer some respite from the west coast weather. The family were therefore very supportive which made both Reg and Phyllis relaxed in the knowledge that their decision to return to Camus in March was well received.

Annie, Craig, Ellie and William were already planning a second visit during the school summer holidays. Ryan was due some leave in March and agreed that it was time, he too, visited to see what all the fuss was about. His best friend Devden from the unit would come with him and they would be happy to help Reg to fit out the intended bunkhouse.

Over the Christmas period they followed up on Ryan's thoughts about camping pods. According to English planning law they are treated much the same as a caravan. Initial research on the internet showed that they cost around £7k each and could earn nightly rental of between £30 and £40. Reg sent all the details to Angus to ask whether he thought that the idea would be considered suitable for Camus and whether it would sit comfortably with the locals. They looked at £35 a night for 100 nights as a conservative model which would give them a return of approx £3500 meaning that they could break even by the end of year two. Donnie was particularly keen as he saw camping pods as complementing his growing kayak business. The alternative was to convert the steading to a dry area for use by all the campers to cook, eat and socialise. They would need to lay on electricity and water but by using their own labour, the cost would probably be less than even one camping pod. Donnie preferred this option, offering their younger guests a real retreat in the rain and a facility not available on other nearby camp sites.

He still talked to others, who had been to Camus before, on Facebook and the feedback he received was encouraging so plans were made to have the steading converted by mid-April, in preparation for the campers expected from May onwards. Angus had arranged for an architect who he had used for his own home to draw up plans. Being local he had a good rapport with the planning department and the building surveyor, which could prove useful. The plans included a drying room for the campers and a kitchen-diner come social room which would be available to all the guests. The plans were submitted in January and, assuming that they would be passed, the work could take place throughout March. This would give them a tight schedule, which Reg would supervise making sure that the finished facility would be ready for the arrival of their first campers.

The previous October, Elaine had launched a web site for Donnie and his kayak business. He had already had a handful of enquiries for the following year. The pages included a gallery of photos taken the previous summer, showing images of youngsters undertaking tuition and racing with excited expressions on their faces. There were images of the field set aside for campers and a link from the Camus site whose facilities were available. Phyllis could report that she had already received enquiries from several people regarding bookings for the forthcoming season. These included a promise of a return from Mick and Maureen, Geoffrey and Ronnie and also the Cole family. They had enquired about a booking for just three. Reg and Phyllis had assumed that the two teenage girls, now older, would not be coming and that Max would surely now be about nine or ten.

Their plans for the steading had been passed on 28th January and so Reg was keen to get an early start. February passed by without even a notice. Soon Reg and Phyllis were, once again loading up the car for the long now familiar drive north only this time there was renewed excitement for the start of their first independent season.

AN INNER CALM

THEY ARRIVED AT Meg's on 20th February, allowing just over a week to spring- clean and set up their caravan and clear out all the old contents from deep inside the steading. Obviously Fergal would now have to be found a new home. Reg had finally finished the restoration the previous season. It was his pride and joy, with newly painted panels, reclaimed tyres and fully working parts. The mere thought of simply covering him with a tarpaulin was a veritable insult and so the space allocated to their caravan during the winter in the corrugated metal shed was the most suitable option. This might well present a problem the following winter but they knew they had almost eight months before they would have to worry.

Reg uncharacteristically had never fully investigated the accumulation of long- forgotten items which took up the far end of the steading. Having discovered the old Fordson his attention had been somewhat diverted so he had only cleared the necessary space. This time he adopted a more thorough approach, allocating an area for obvious debris suitable only for the bonfire, another area for tools which might come in handy, another for re-useable material and another for 'don't know', in other words curiosities worthy of further investigation. He donned his trusty blue overalls and set to.

Outside, a familiar visitor appeared, head poking through the door, tentative but curious. It was Norman who had obviously heard the clattering coming from inside the steading and was keen to check that his dustbin of pellets was still intact. Perhaps he was hoping that a few stray treats would head in his direction. He still had an even thicker winter coat, although Reg had noticed that there was little distinction between his long coat in summer or winter. According to Angus, Tormad was a particularly fine specimen. His coat was fairly straight with only the slightest hint of a curl around his shoulders; his forelock was thick, extending down past his eyes. However Reg was convinced that this had never prevented him from seeing new caravans from a fair distance as they approach the site.

"Hello Tormad" Reg called out "So nice to see you again. I suppose you've come to see what I'm up to."

Although he had moved 'the dustbin' to one side for safe keeping he couldn't resist encouraging Tormad to step further inside by scattering a pile of pellets in a trail across the floor. Reg kind of liked the company as Phyllis had declined the offer to assist for fear of the 'beasties' which Reg was sure to disturb.

Phyllis and Meg had headed back to the mainland to stock up with food for the freezer and supplies for the site shop. They would be gone for the whole day based on previous similar excursions. So Reg and Tormad were left alone to explore the steading, the only inconvenience being that Reg had scattered too many pellets near the door thereby causing Tormad to block the exit and hence Reg's access to his carefully pre-planned areas.

The debris pile rose quickly, with old sacks and feed bags evidence that the steading had indeed been used to store food for the animals in earlier days. The floor was compacted with animal dung which had fortunately long lost its aroma but would need digging out before a new screed floor was laid. There were old forks and spades and scythes which were almost certainly in use before Fergal's time. Reg kept the scythes which he could use around the edges of the site but the old forks and spades had seen better days. The wooden handles were broken or weakened through time and so reluctantly they were also added to the debris pile Reg having, of course, first removed the metal parts not destined for a bonfire. He was so pleased whenever an item was added to the curiosity pile. He thought that he would ask Angus's father, Hamish, if he knew what these strange implements were and whether he had ever used them.

In the far corner were two large, rounded stones which had clearly not been displaced from the steading walls. They were both very heavy and rather covered in ancient cow dung but Reg was still a strong, fit man and managed to carry out each one, carefully placing it separately to the side of the curiosity pile. He was particularly excited about these finds and was keen to research more but, as expected, he did not allow himself to be overly distracted from his objective to clear the contents completely.

Meg had kindly made him a packed lunch and Phyllis had prepared a flask of tea so when it came to midday he looked forward to a rest and sat down outside. Tormad casually made his way outside too, having exhausted the supply of pellets that Reg had provided. He had obviously seen enough of the activity as he wandered off across the field to check out the rest of his territory. Reg always looked forward to Megs sandwiches, or 'pieces' as she called them, and in particular her home-made bread. Today it was lovely thick ham oozing with her own onion chutney. After lunch he afforded himself a leisurely stroll around the site.

It was a typically inspiring day, the air was still quite cold and crisp but the sky was clear and blue. The sound of oyster catchers once again filled the air and several were foraging in the kelp lined up along the shore. As he looked across the Sound, the now familiar skyline of the islands rose from the sea, awaiting the return of seabirds to find just the right spot for their nests. A familiar dishevelled-looking heron stood on the shoreline, poised motionless for his next catch. It was hard for Reg to resist the temptation to linger and absorb but as usual he had a long schedule of tasks which needed to be set in motion in preparation for the start of their planned refurbishment and indeed their new, independent season.

Having emptied all the contents of the steading, Reg was surprised at how much space there actually was. The plans drawn by Angus's friend revealed the overall dimensions as 8950 by 5720 but Reg preferred to revert back to imperial equivalents roughly 29ft by 18ft - plenty of room for the planned drying room and kitchen/dining/lounge areas. The roof trusses needed a good clean but were mainly intact. The roof itself had been replaced by corrugated metal many years ago although Reg believed that it was probably once thatched. The plans were to replace the metal roof with a more modern bonded, insulated equivalent, to lay a new screed floor, to re-point all the strong stone walls and create a drying room for the campers to hang their bedraggled clothes. A kitchen was to be built, in which to cook a hot meal and provide a comfortable area to eat and pass the time when the infamous weather forced the campers inside.

Ryan and Devden were expected to arrive on 9th March. They would be staying at Meg's for three weeks whilst helping with the refurbishment. Reg had already planned to visit Angus to get his opinion on the detailed project plan which he had drafted back in Worcester. Elaine had invited them to dinner, asking Meg to join them to ensure that the project included a women's touch. Hamish was also to be there. He was now approaching 87 but was still good for his age. Reg knew that he would love to hear about the progress with the steading and hopefully might shed more light on the curious objects he had uncovered inside.

Elaine's meal was delicious and she had opened a bottle of champagne to toast their arrival and the start of their first, independent season. Phyllis was touched. By now she truly felt part of the local community. Hamish had brought with him some old black and white photos of the steading, which included pictures of his parents tending the croft back in the 1800s. In one picture Reg was excited to see the couple using an implement which looked similar to one he had found but could not work out what it was. They were obviously using it to dig in the ground but Hamish knew more.

"I've found a tool just like that" Reg announced.

Hamish went on to tell him what it was "It's a cas chrom" he revealed "Or as you would say a 'crooked foot'." He then went on to describe it as an old ploughing tool which was particularly suitable for the Highlands because of the rocky ground. As a young boy he had seen his parents use it to prepare the land for the crop of turnips which they used to grow to feed the animals. Now that Reg had found out what it was, he could see that it was indeed similar in shape to a foot. Hamish loved to talk about the old days and went on to explain that the cas chrom was often fabricated by the crofters themselves from available material such as driftwood found on the beaches.

He began to go deeper in to history, telling them that most highland land was farmed and divided on the basis of run rigs, or lazy-beds. Apparently this method of land distribution was often communal, and the layout of the lazy-beds had to accommodate the contours and features of the rugged land. His croft now covered what would have been a series of run rigs. Once reminiscing he went on for what seemed to Phyllis to be hours, talking about his childhood and what he grew on the croft when he was just a lad.

Elaine was obviously prompted to add to the mood by selecting a CD of Gaelic songs by the famous Scots band Runrig.

"Who?" asked Phyllis, confessing that she had never heard of them but Angus assured her that if she spoke to any Scots people they would certainly know. Surely she had heard the Murrayfield crowd singing along to their version of Loch Lomond played at almost every major rugby game? Although she couldn't understand the words she loved the music. Neither Elaine nor Donnie confessed to speaking Gaelic and although Angus knew many words, he could hardly profess to be a fluent Gaelic speaker.

Sadly Hamish didn't have any photos of the steading old enough to show the thatch which he agreed would have once covered the roof. He thought that if indeed it was once thatched it would probably have been covered with heather, which was more common in the Highlands. As far as he could remember, it had always been a cow byre but he suggested that one of the old local historians, also called Angus, might have more information based on the often incomplete records of the old census data going back long before his time.

When Reg described the two rounded stones he had also put aside, Hamish once again did not disappoint.

"Och they would be a 'quern" he said now revelling in his centre stage importance. Only too often the older people are expected to sit quietly in the corner often excluded from the conversation enjoyed by the younger members of the company.

Meg now also joined in "My mother had a quern just outside the door. I remember it well."

According to Hamish a 'quern' was a type of hand mill, a device for grinding grain between two circular pieces of stone. In the lower stone, there was often a wooden peg, rounded at the top, on which the upper stone would have balanced, so as to just touch the lower one. This would have left room for feeding the mill, allowing some friction from the contact of the two stones, and yet a very small momentum made it revolve several times, even when it had no corn in it. Two women would sit down on the ground, having the quern between them. One would feed it, while the other turned it around; they would relieve each other, occasionally singing some Celtic songs or so he had read. Hamish was painting a picture of such an idyllic, long- forgotten tradition that all the guests were now giving him their full attention.

"Wouldn't it be nice if these old tools were on display in the steading" suggested Meg. Her comment prompted a wider discussion as to whether they should be displayed in the steading or the site reception or even offered to a local museum.

For the time being everyone agreed that they should remain at Camus. Elaine, along with Paige and Camran, would design information boards, telling visitors about the implements and history.

Reg shared the next few days between ordering materials for the steading and those required in the normal course of preparing the site. He knew that when Ryan and Devden came it would be all hands to the pump. The more jobs he could therefore do around the site at this early stage, the more relaxed he would feel.

When the boys arrived, Reg and Phyllis couldn't wait to show them around the site. Ryan had heard so much about their venture but he soon confessed that it was better than he'd imagined. The boys were both used to travelling but agreed that this part of Britain beat most of the scenery they had experienced so far. The air was still cold and the ground hard but some strenuous digging would soon warm them up.

The plan of action was first to lay the electricity and water supplies, then to replace the roof, affording them respite from the endless rain they had, by now, learnt to expect. There were to be windows both in the drying room and the kitchen diner. These had been ordered and were expected within the next few days. Reg intended to put a false ceiling above the drying room, which would be at the far end, below the rafters upon which the barn owl had previously nested. Since Reg had cleared the steading, the owl had not been seen but he hoped that by leaving a suitable spot it might return when all the works were complete and still left the same exit in the far wall from which the owl was known to emerge.

Ryan and Devden got on famously with Donnie, who seemed to look upon them both with admiration. He, too, had offered to help as it was particularly with his future clients in mind that the plans had been drafted. The kayaking season was yet to start but the three boys had already planned to wait for a good day before Donnie would take them out on the sea. They took a day to settle in at Meg's and take a tour of the immediate area but on the second day they started to dig the trench for utilities. The ground was hard and full of stones and rocks but they were used to hard graft. Ryan was anticipating constant instruction from his father but little came. Reg could clearly see that the lads' army training ensured that they knew exactly what was required.

Once the cables and pipes were laid, their next task was to remove the corrugated metal roof and prepare to fix the new panels. Of course, Tormad put in an appearance each day as if to check on progress. Ryan had heard so much about him from his parents and also from Ellie, who recounted the bed time stories told by Meg. Devden had never seen a Highlander before and was quite taken by his strong, confident manner.

Over the next two weeks they worked hard to secure the new roof, carefully removed some stones to install a new window and re-pointing all the walls. They had installed a welcoming wood burner for the campers to use, adding a cosy feeling to the social room ready for when the weather was bad. Finally the new screed floor was laid and left to dry. There was still a basic kitchen to fit and some furniture to be bought and installed but Reg, Donnie and Angus had agreed to do the rest. There was still a week to go before the site's opening on 2nd April but Reg was pleased with the progress they had all made.

Unfortunately the lads were due to return to their unit so it wasn't possible for them to share a final farewell in the finished steading. Meg however kindly agreed to host a small dinner party at her house. Reg and Phyllis were due to take them back to the airport the following day but were so pleased when the lads promised to return on their next leave home.

As soon as the work was finished, Elaine suggested that they add some pictures to the website. She took some lovely photos, including one of the drying room with suitably selected clothes hanging from a creel suspended high up in the ceiling, one of the kitchen/dining area with Donnie and friends eating and laughing at the table and one of the wood burner complete with roaring logs. Phyllis felt sure that this new facility would become a real draw to their camping clients.

There were now only three days to go until the start of the season. They were both really looking forward to seeing Mick and Maureen and Geoffrey and Ronnie and also all the new, interesting people they could expect to meet this year. No longer were they nervous as 2nd April arrived, instead they both felt an inner calm and a real sense of belonging. Camus was certainly a peaceful, happy place and, at that moment, they both agreed there was no-where else on earth where they would rather be.

ABOUT THE AUTHOR

Jessie MacQuarrie was born in Southern England not far from the busy hustle and bustle of London. Her love of the great outdoors started at an early age. One lasting memory goes back to a family holiday in Scotland at about the age of eight. Whilst filling a camping kettle at the foot of Ben Nevis she asked her parents whether they could climb the mountain. The response, at that time, was negative but in later years she and her husband scaled many peaks including Scafell, Snowdon and indeed Ben Nevis.

Her successful career as a qualified accountant lasted many years but she always felt happiest walking for hours in beautiful parts of Britain and in particular Scotland. Sadly in 2010 she was diagnosed with Multiple Sclerosis and, as a result, her ability to continue hill walking quickly diminished. She retired from work but refused to accept that her passion for the outdoors had also ended.

Her husband's great grandmother always spoke so fondly of the beautiful island of Ulva just off Mull on Scotland's west coast. Touring initially in their 28 year old VW camper they visited the island and have since returned many times. Inspired by the old lady's recollections they have researched much of the history of Mull, Ulva and the Western Isles.

They now own a touring caravan which affords them the chance to stay on idyllic sites surrounded by spectacular views and majestic wildlife. Multiple Sclerosis may have closed one door but the pleasure to be had from the landscape is always there to see and appreciate.

Adjusting to life without a stressful job has afforded Jessie the opportunity to write a story based partly on her knowledge and partly on her experience. The book includes characters both human and animal. It contains stories which may well strike a chord with those who share Jessie's love of both Scotland and of caravan touring.